STORM

Survival in the Land of the Dead

SHAUN HARBINGER

Storm: A Zombie Novel
Copyright © 2014 Shaun Harbinger
All rights reserved.

All characters are works of fiction. Any resemblance to real persons living, dead or undead is purely coincidental.

Also Available
Rain

One

A THICK GREY FOG CLUNG to the hull of *The Big Easy*, making it impossible to see anything beyond. As I stood on the sun deck looking toward the bow, sinuous tendrils snaked over my boots. The air was cold and wet and the chill seeped into my bones. We drifted aimlessly, the boat bobbing up and down beneath my feet, gentle waves rocking us like a mother trying to persuade her baby to sleep.

But the only lullaby was a far-off cry of gulls, and the chilly dawn air dispelled any thoughts of comfort.

The bed I had climbed out of half an hour earlier was comfortable. There, I could snuggle beneath the blankets with Lucy and dream of a better time.

A time when my friends were still alive and the world had not yet tipped into the deepest region of hell.

A dream that had startled me awake. There was no way I was going to get back to sleep after that. I had dreamed of my brother, Joe, and my parents sitting in a cage in a dense forest. I was running toward the cage, determined to break them free. But as I approached, the forest suddenly became alive with shambling figures hell-bent on stopping me. Alive wasn't the right word. They were undead.

As the dream-zombies shuffled closer to me, I snapped my eyes open and realized I was still on *The Big Easy*. No more sleep. So I came up to the deck to stand in the cold fog and think about my next move.

Not the greatest idea of my life. The "Sail To Your Destiny" T-shirt I wore did nothing to protect me from the dawn chill. The insidious fog made the fabric damp and clingy. My face and arms felt like they were covered in droplets of ice.

I wondered if the fog reached to wherever Joe was. A few days ago, I heard his voice on Survivor Reach Out and now I was possessed of one single thought: I had to save him. He was somewhere on the mainland, in a Survivors Camp, and that meant danger. I had already seen what happens in those camps.

The problem was, I had no idea which camp my family was in. And even if I found out, how was I going to break them out of what was basically a military-run prison?

The task of rescuing Joe seemed so impossible, I didn't know where to start. When I had heard his voice on Survivor Radio, I had turned *The Big Easy* to shore, ready to storm the beaches and fight the zombies, but Lucy had pointed out the foolishness of that idea. I had reluctantly agreed and piloted the boat south along the coast. It was only when I saw the familiar coastline of Wales and the dark buildings of the city of Swansea that I stopped the boat and let us drift overnight.

Now, as I stood on the sundeck, I had no idea how far we were from Swansea. Mike had taught me the basics of piloting the boat but nothing about navigation. The coastline was completely obscured by the fog.

The cold, damp air was too uncomfortable and the chill made me shiver. I went inside the living area and closed the wooden door. I switched on the radiators and put the kettle on. A cup of tea wasn't going to make anything better but it might warm up my insides.

The small door that led to the bedrooms opened and Lucy poked her head around it, looking for me with bleary blue eyes. Her blonde hair was sticking out and an oversized "Sail To Your Destiny" T-shirt hid her curves but she was still beautiful. As "just got out of bed" looks went, she had the best.

"Why are you up so early?" she asked as she came into the living area and sank down onto the sofa.

"Couldn't sleep. You want a drink?"

"Coffee." She looked out at the fog. "Wow."

"Yeah," I said, "the weather's really closed in. Can't see anything out there." I made the drinks and passed her a mug of coffee while my tea bag brewed in the cup. I wanted it strong and hot. My skin still felt wet and clammy. I needed warmth.

"You come up with any plans?" Lucy asked. We both knew I hadn't. What plan could possibly be made other than the plan to go ashore and look for Joe?

Maybe that was the answer. Simple and direct.

And probably fatal.

I looked at the impenetrable grey fog beyond the windows and wondered if I could use it to my advantage somehow. The fog was made up of droplets of moisture so the zombies would probably avoid it just as they avoided rain. It might be safe to go ashore just so long as I avoided the military patrols. The fog could help me with that. If I couldn't see them, they couldn't see me and I could move undetected.

It all sounded so easy but my heart hammered at the thought of sneaking around on the mainland. Too much could go wrong. What if the fog lifted while I was standing among a hundred soldiers? What if zombies wandered in the fog and I went blindly blundering into a group of them?

What choice did I have? If I was going to rescue Joe and my parents, I had to go ashore at some point. The fog provided the best chance of survival.

"I'm going to go ashore," I told Lucy.

"What? Don't be crazy, Alex. You have no idea where your brother is. Until you know more…"

"How am I going to know more unless I look for him? Floating out here all day isn't doing anybody any good."

"At least we're safe."

"Are we? What if we run into pirates? Or a boat full of zombies hits us and they get on board? Nowhere is safe anymore."

"But wandering onto the mainland where there are thousands of zombies and soldiers is suicide."

"I'll be careful," I said. "I won't go far from shore. I just want to get an idea of the situation. A reconnaissance mission."

She shook her head and gave me a thin-lipped smile. "You hate the military, remember? You're no soldier, Alex."

I knew that. If playing military video games counted toward an army rank, I'd be a colonel by now but in reality, I was overweight and slow… the result of spending all my leisure time playing video games. Ironic. I could kill a base full of digital terrorists on my console but in real life I was nothing more than a walking target.

I was honestly surprised I was still alive in this post-apocalyptic world. Much better people than me had fallen already. I thought of Mike and Elena and felt a hollowness in my stomach.

Gulping down the hot tea didn't help.

I had come to a decision. No matter how much Lucy tried to talk me out of it, I was going ashore under cover of the fog.

Not too far inland.

What could go wrong?

Two

"THIS IS CRAZY, ALEX," LUCY informed me as we sailed slowly through the fog, looking for the coast. She stood on the aft deck below me, arms folded, as I sat in the small chair on *The Big Easy's* bridge and peered out of the window at the thick, grey impenetrable gloom beyond the bow. I had tried putting on the boat's lights but they had just reflected off the wall of fog. Useless.

I kept my hand on the throttle, ready to pull it back if I saw any shapes beyond our bow. My greatest fear was running into unseen rocks and destroying our boat. We barely crawled along but even so, my hands were shaking and my nerves were on edge. I had thrown on a hoodie and felt insulated against the cold fog but I wasn't sure if the sweat running down my back and chest was because I was warm or scared. Probably both.

Lucy had a right to be mad at me. I wasn't just risking my own life with this stupid move; I was risking both our lives and *The Big Easy*. But I was sure the fog would give me the best chance to move about onshore unseen. If I wasted this opportunity, I would be kicking myself forever.

Something dark appeared ahead. I yanked the throttle back and the engines went into reverse, churning the water at the stern. Lucy leaned over the side and gazed ahead to see what had caused my reaction.

A dark shape jutted out into the water like a bony finger. I turned the wheel to steer us clear and saw a second identical shape farther away.

"It's the marina jetties," Lucy said.

This was perfect. We needed a rowboat to get to and from shore easily. We could pick one up here then sail to a more remote part of the coast. I could row ashore while Lucy stayed with *The Big Easy*. I started to feel more optimistic about the plan.

"We can get fuel and a rowboat," I said. "We don't need to stay here long." I guided the boat along the weathered wooden jetty. Through the fog, I could see the bulky dark shapes of moored boats bobbing on the gentle waves. I cut the engine. Lucy jumped onto the jetty with our mooring rope and tied us off when we reached the fuel pump.

I climbed down the ladder to the aft deck and grabbed my baseball bat. "I won't be long," I said as I passed Lucy, who was already operating the fuel pump. She didn't reply. I couldn't blame her for being angry.

The wooden slats creaked beneath my boots. I held the bat loosely in my hands and crept along slowly, knowing that if there was anyone else on this jetty, I wouldn't see them until they were a few feet in front of me. I risked a glance backward. *The Big Easy* was no more than a dark shape in the grey. I couldn't see Lucy.

I peered at each slip I passed, looking for a rowboat. The boats here were mainly pleasure craft, used for fishing weekends or excursions out to sea on sunny days. Some of them belonged to the marina and were hired out to casual boaters. These boats had the slogan "Sail To Your Destiny" painted on the hull beneath the boats' name and number.

A few fishing vessels were among them, littered with lobster traps and nets, working boats whose work was done forever. Most of these craft would never go out to sea again. Their owners were either dead or shambling around the city looking for human prey, thoughts of sunny pleasure trips far from their rotted minds.

I didn't find a rowboat until I reached the shore. There, sitting on the pebbled beach beneath the marine supply store, sat a tidy-looking pale yellow wooden boat complete with oars stowed under the seats. She was flooded with rainwater but I could tip that out and be rowing back to *The Big Easy* in no time.

I dropped from the jetty and went over to the yellow boat. The pebbles made a crunching sound beneath my boots. It sounded too loud in the otherwise quiet fog-enshrouded morning. If anybody was around, I had just given away my location.

Standing by the boat, my hands gripping the smooth wood of the baseball bat tightly, I listened. All I could hear was my own breathing and the soft whisper of the waves lapping up onto the pebbles. A far off clunking sound told me Lucy had replaced the fuel line onto the pumping machine. *The big Easy* was fuelled and ready to go.

So was I. My noisy trek across the pebbles had unnerved me. I wanted to get out of here. Now.

I wasn't even sure I wanted to come ashore again today, even under cover of the fog. The lack of visibility suddenly felt dangerous. There could be a herd of zombies standing on this beach only a few feet from me and I wouldn't even know it until they reached for me.

Enough scaring myself. I needed to leave.

I laid the bat on the pebbles and gripped the edge of the rowboat, pulling up with all my strength to tip out the accumulated water. It sloshed noisily around inside but it made the boat too heavy to tip. Great. Just great. I stood and stretched my aching back then squatted down and placed my hands against the slippery hull of the rowboat.

Pushing with my legs, I managed to move it over onto its side far enough that water came flooding out onto the pebbles. The oars clattered loudly against the inner hull.

I heard another sound: footsteps crunching on the pebbles behind me. Rapid and rhythmic. Not zombies. But probably still as dangerous.

I dropped the boat as quietly as I could but the oars banged against the hull again.

The footsteps increased their pace toward me.

I looked toward the jetty. I could run back to *The Big Easy* but what if they followed me? We couldn't untie the boat and be underway before they had a chance to get on board. At the moment, *The Big Easy* and Lucy were safe in the shroud of fog. I wanted to keep it that way.

Picking up the bat, I crept across the pebbles to the cement walkway in front of the marine store and crouched there, flattening myself against the rough brick wall. I was too exposed here. I could still see the rowboat, which meant if anyone stood there, they could see me.

The footsteps were getting louder.

I pushed on the glass door to the marine supply store and slipped inside. Something touched my neck and I thought for a terrifying moment that I had stumbled into a zombie but it was just a wetsuit hanging on a rail. I sat in the darkness and tried to calm myself down. My breathing sounded so loud I was sure anyone outside the store would be able to hear it.

The footsteps stopped and I heard voices. Men's voices. I couldn't make out the words through the door. I wished I had hidden further back among the shelves of the store. What if they came in here? I was so close to the glass door, they would trip over me.

I inched across the cold tiled floor looking for a hiding place. The store had been the source of the clothes I now wore and it looked like it had been looted by others as well. The clothing racks were almost bare and most of them had been tipped over onto the floor. The wooden shelves that ran down the center of the store had been pushed over and lay in pieces like broken bones on the hard floor.

Sliding back into the shadows at the back of the store, I tried to avoid the splinters of wood and lengths of chrome rails. I had to be silent. Sitting in the dark, leaning back against the wall, I tried to control my breathing.

I waited there for at least five minutes, bat clutched tightly in my hands, before I dared move back to the door. I peered through the dirty glass.

The fog had lifted slightly. On the pebbles, the yellow rowboat sat alone, waiting for me. I had to get out of here. Lucy was right; coming ashore here was a stupid idea. As soon as I rowed that little yellow boat to *The Big Easy*, I was never going to come back to this city again.

There was no sign of the men I had heard.

I opened the door and slowly put my head out, listening.

All I could hear was the whisper of gentle waves rolling over the pebbles and the distant rumblings of engines somewhere in the city. I stepped outside. The baseball bat felt heavy. I didn't want to use it on living people but I would if they stood between me and *The Big Easy*.

I strode quickly to the rowboat, grabbed the cold damp wooden edge of the stern, and dragged it across the pebbles toward the sea. The cold water ran into my boots and soaked the bottom of my jeans as I waded in to better pull the boat into water deep enough to float it.

Satisfied that the boat wouldn't touch the bottom even when it held my weight, I threw the bat in and clambered after it. By the time I was in the rowboat, I was wet, cold and breathing hard. I didn't have time to take a breather; I was barely six feet from the shore. If the waves took me any closer to the beach, I'd be grounded. I didn't want to get into the freezing water again to push the boat farther out.

I picked up one of the wet oars and slid the blade into the water to push the boat out to sea. The oar sank into the pebbles on the sea bed. I put my weight against it and pushed. The boat moved farther out from shore.

I dragged the oar back in and pushed it into the metal oar lock on the side of the boat. It went in with a loud *clunk*.

Reaching for the second oar, I glanced toward the shore and froze with fear.

Two men were running out of the fog toward me. Their clothes were filthy and torn, their faces gaunt and bearded. In the old world, I would have assumed they were homeless.

In this new world they were simply survivors. They probably spent every day avoiding the army and zombies, scavenging for food and taking what they needed to survive for one more day.

One of them held a meat cleaver, the other a hand axe.

Their eyes were wild.

STORM

They splashed into the water and grabbed the boat, raising their weapons.

I picked up my bat and prepared to fight for my life.

Three

AS THEY GRABBED THE BOAT, it rocked violently from side to side and my boots slipped on the slick wood. I lost my balance and fell headfirst into the sea. The world became a rush of deathly-cold water as I went under. I fought for air, finding the loose pebble bed beneath my boots and pushing against it until my face broke the surface and I breathed in a lungful of cold air, standing waist deep in the sea.

The man closest to me swung the hand axe at my head. He had to wade into deeper water to reach me and the waves pushed at him, spoiling his swing. I lifted the baseball bat with both hands and blocked the blow. As the axe shaft hit the hard wood of the bat, I pulled back, yanking the axe out of the wild survivor's hand. His weapon dropped into the sea between us with a splash.

Wild-eyed, he lunged at me.

I barely had time to get the bat between us. He grabbed it and tried to wrestle it out of my hands.

His companion was getting closer, coming around the rowboat with the cleaver held high.

I needed to move.

Now.

I jabbed the bat forward into the survivor's face. His nose exploded and he let go of the bat to put his hands to his face. I used that split second to kick out into deeper water. The bat encumbered me and I was no Olympic swimmer but I had no other option. If I went for the beach they would outrun me and pull me down to the ground. Swimming out to sea was the only chance I had.

If I could just make it to *The Big Easy* with enough distance between me and the pursuing survivor, I could climb on board to safety.

I glanced over my shoulder. The man behind me moved through the waves with choppy strokes of his arms, his bloodshot eyes wild as he realised his prey might escape.

I faced forward again and pulled myself through the water in a combination of breaststroke and front crawl. I hated swimming. My parents used to take Joe and me to the local pool once a week when we were kids but it soon lost its appeal. As I got older, I drifted into the world of video games and the only swimming I participated in was on a game console.

Exhaustion hit me like a heavy weight, threatening to pull me under. Panicking, I looked behind me. The wild survivor was gaining on me.

I wouldn't make it to *The Big Easy*.

Looking around, I spotted a chrome ladder on the side of the jetty. As I made for it, I squinted against the fog in an attempt to see our boat but I couldn't see her through the grey wall. We would need to be underway as soon as I reached her, before the two survivors got on board and killed us in their crazy rage.

I reached the ladder and put my boot on the rungs below the water, pulling myself up despite the tiredness and cold.

I shouted toward the end of the jetty as I climbed. "Lucy! We need to get out of here! Untie the boat!"

Exhausted, I reached the top of the ladder and crawled onto the wooden slats of the jetty as my pursuer reached the bottom of the ladder. This was going to be tight. Would I even make it?

A moan escaped my lips as I scrambled to my feet and staggered toward the end of the jetty in a slow run.

"Lucy!" I called, "Start the engines!" It was too quiet. If the yacht's engines were running, I should be able to hear them. I had to be close enough now.

All I could hear was rapid footsteps behind me. They beat on the wood like a drum counting off the final seconds of my life.

I pushed myself to run faster. If I could just get to *The Big Easy*, I had more of a fighting chance. Lucy was there and she had weapons, including the gun.

Run!

The footsteps were louder, closer. I could hear the survivor's ragged breath, smell his sweat mixed with salty sea water.

The fuel pump appeared through the thick fog.

I looked for *The Big Easy* but there was no reassuring bulky dark shape where she had been moored.

Just empty sea.

The Big Easy…and Lucy…were gone.

Four

THE EDGE OF THE JETTY appeared but I couldn't stop. The man behind me was so close I had already braced myself to feel the razor-sharp edge of the meat cleaver slicing through my skin. I ran until the wood beneath my boots disappeared and I was falling towards the water, trying to grab a breath of air in my burning lungs before I went under.

The coldness enveloped me in a sudden rush and I fought my way to the surface. My lungs felt like they were on fire. The muscles in my arms barely held enough strength to pull me through the water.

I took a deep gulp of air and checked the water around me. No sign of my pursuer. I looked up at the jetty. He wasn't there either. Maybe he hadn't followed me into the water. He could have given up and gone back to check on his companion.

I trod water and got my breath back, taking in deep lungsful of chilly, moist air. I couldn't stay out here much longer; I was already tiring. It would be ironic if I managed to escape a cleaver-wielding maniac only to drown in the sea.

Swimming back to the marina was out of the question; they could be waiting there for me. I had to swim across to the beach and pray the coast was clear.

As I kicked out and tried to relax into an easy breaststroke, I cursed myself for leaving the safety of *The Big Easy*. Lucy had been right; my plan was stupid. If I had listened to her, I would be on board right now drinking hot coffee instead of swimming in the icy sea.

My life was in danger. Alone and onshore, I had very little chance of survival. I had stupidly thought the fog would protect me but instead it had separated me from Lucy and the safety of our boat. Once the fog faded, I would be visible to both the military and the shambling nasties.

I wasn't sure which I feared most.

After a few minutes of swimming, I headed toward the beach. The sun had burned off some of the fog and I could see the stretch of sand and the dark angle of the cliffs. The beach looked deserted.

If I could hole up there for half an hour, I could then double back and take a boat. Once I was safely at sea, I could search for Lucy. All I needed to do was wait thirty minutes or so and hope the two crazy survivors had moved on from the marina. With nothing there to kill or steal, I assumed they would lose interest and search elsewhere for victims.

I swam into the shallows and reached down with my legs, finding the soft sand. Wading through the chest-high cold water, trying to move faster despite the shifting sand beneath my boots, I scanned the beach. No movement other than a pair of seagulls fighting over the carcass of a dead fish.

The sand beneath my feet sloped upwards and I struggled up onto the beach. I stumbled out of the water and collapsed onto my back, staring up at the grey sky. I was exhausted. Every muscle ached and my breath came in harsh gasps that burned my throat. I wasn't built for this kind of physical action. Although I had lost a few pounds since the apocalypse, I was still out of shape and unfit.

That could get me killed, especially in this situation.

I sat up and looked for somewhere to lie low. There were caves in the cliffs. If I could hide inside one of those and…

Something burst from the sea in a spray of water. I turned in time to see the wild-eyed survivor with the meat cleaver running through the shallows towards me.

I barely had time to think. Reflexively, I grabbed the bat from the damp sand and struggled to my feet. He reached me in seconds, raising the cleaver high above his head as he prepared to deal me the death blow.

I didn't want to die. Not here on this wet, fog-enshrouded beach.

I swung the bat.

It connected with his stomach, doubling him over. He let go of the cleaver but its forward momentum carried it in a deadly arc towards my head.

I ducked and it whistled past me in the air before landing with a dull *thud* in the sand.

The survivor was on his knees, struggling to his feet.

I couldn't let that happen. He had followed me all the way from the marina with murderous intent. As long as he lived, I would be hunted.

I swung the baseball bat down onto the back of his neck. The cracking sound it made as it connected with his spine sickened me. This wasn't a zombie. This was a human being. A survivor.

Not anymore.

He lay in the sand. Silent. Still.

At least he was face down. I couldn't bear to see his eyes staring up at me.

I walked away from the body quickly, leaving his cleaver half buried in the sand. Hopefully, the tide would come in soon and wash everything away.

As I looked for caves in the cliff wall, the sound of vehicles and voices reached me through the fog. They sounded far off but I quickened my search.

When I found a narrow crack that was barely wide enough to crawl into, I peered inside. It ran deep enough into the cliffs that it was pitch black in there. I sniffed the air. Sand, salt and seaweed. No sickly-sweet stench of death.

I crawled inside, feeling my way along the rough rock walls. The cave was small and dark but at least it was hidden from the beach. And I was sure it was far enough from the water's edge to escape the high tide. The sand in here was dry.

I leaned back against the wall and closed my eyes. This was a bad day. My simple plan to come ashore and find a rowboat had quickly unravelled and now I had no idea where Lucy was or how I was going to get back to *The Big Easy*. Why had Lucy left the marina? Why had she abandoned me? There had to be a good reason. She wouldn't have left me just because she was mad at me for going ashore. Would she?

Of course she wouldn't. Lucy knew how dangerous it was on foot, how difficult to survive without the sea between us and the nasties. She would never leave me alone here.

At the moment, her reason didn't matter. Knowing why she left the marina wasn't going to help me get a boat and sail out to find her. I needed to focus on the here and now while I still had a here and now to focus on.

The noises of men and vehicles were louder. Voices drifted on the breeze along with the clanking of heavy machinery. It was still far enough away that I didn't have to worry but what if one of those men decided to take a walk along the beach and found the body lying on the sand? What if that made them wary, compelled them to search the area?

My hiding place suddenly seemed exposed. I was trapped inside this tiny hole in the rocks.

I tried to calm myself down but I couldn't resist the urge to look outside and check the beach. If I saw people coming this way, I could run.

Crawling outside, I pressed myself against the rocks and squinted against the fog. The sun had burned most of it away and I could see all the way to the marina. What I saw there made my heart sink.

The place was crawling with soldiers and military vehicles. They had a big rumbling excavator belching smoke and gouging trenches in the sand with its steel bucket. Land Rovers and armoured personnel carriers were parked on the beach and around the marina. Soldiers scurried along the jetties carrying sandbags and large pieces of metal. There was even a tank sitting there, its gun barrel pointing across the beach at me like an accusing finger.

I was sure they hadn't seen me yet but I couldn't stay here with the army crawling over the area. There was no way I could get a boat from the marina now.

What the hell was I going to do?

Keeping close to the rocks, I headed in the opposite direction along the cliffs. A quick glance over my shoulder now and then told me they hadn't seen me. They were too busy doing their job, whatever that was.

The beach ahead of me terminated at a large cliff that jutted into the sea. A set of sun-bleached stone steps flanked by grey metal handrails led up to the cliff top. I didn't want to go up there. The streets of the city were deadly.

But I couldn't stay here and wait to be discovered by the soldiers who had invaded the beach. Besides, the tide was coming in and I was already wet and cold.

I walked over the steps but hesitated. The fog had disappeared. Any advantage it might have given me was gone. It was a sunny morning, which meant the zombies would be roaming the streets. I hadn't wanted this. Why hadn't I listened to Lucy and stayed aboard *The Big Easy*?

Wondering how many more dumb decisions I was going to make and if any of them were going to cost me my life, I put my boot on the first step and wrapped my fingers around the cold metal handrail.

As slow as a man walking to the gas chamber, I went up to the city.

Five

BY THE TIME I GOT to the top of the steps, the sky had cleared and the sun was beating down, making steam rise from my wet clothes. I cast a nervous glance around. An overgrown grassy area in front of me led to a coastal road that wound around the cliff tops. Across the road, a row of three-storey houses, some of which had been made into inns, looked empty.

I crawled into the grass, my head turning left and right as I tried to take in all of my surroundings. The noises from the soldiers at the marina were faint now. I could hear far away shambling sounds, which I was sure must be zombies coming out of hiding but I couldn't tell how many there were or their location.

I felt exposed out here in the grass, vulnerable. Across the road, a number of cars were parked outside the houses.

If I could get a vehicle, I would feel safer. I could leave the city, drive somewhere remote and decide what to do next. I couldn't make any decisions while I was in danger of being killed by a herd of nasties or thrown into a Survivors Camp by the army. I couldn't think of anything except my immediate self-preservation.

I ran across the road, keeping low, and rested between two parked cars. Logic told me that if the cars were parked here outside their owners' homes, the car keys were somewhere in the houses.

Along with the owners. Alive or dead. Either way, they were a danger to me.

The house closest to me had a wooden porch painted in flaking eggshell blue paint. The sun and salty air had taken their toll on the house's exterior, eating at the wooden window frames and fading the paint until it looked like a sun-bleached skull covered in flaking pieces of bone.

I broke cover and went up the steps to the porch. It creaked beneath my boots. The front door was made of wood painted in the same pale blue and had two panels of frosted glass running down each side. I put my hand on the rusted metal handle and tried the door.

Locked.

Using the tip of the baseball bat, I broke the pane of glass nearest the handle and reached inside, hoping the key was in the lock. If not, I would have to try another house.

STORM

My searching fingers found a bunch of keys hanging from the lock. I felt for the key that was in the door, found it and turned it. The lock clicked and the door opened.

I stepped inside, glad to be off the street. But the stench that hit me made me wonder if I was safer outside.

The smell of rancid meat hung in the air.

Trying not to puke, I readied the bat and made a quick assessment of the place. The hallway and stairs were covered in thick grass-green carpet. The wallpaper was pale lime. Someone sure liked green.

Was that someone still here?

To my left, an open doorway revealed a living room. There was a TV and leather furniture in there but no movement. Ahead of me, a doorway led to the kitchen. I could see a small white microwave sitting on the counter but the rest of the room was out of sight. I could hear the high-pitched buzzing of a swarm of flies in there.

I crept forward slowly, the plush carpet muffling my footsteps.

I peered around the edge of the doorway. There was nothing in there except an oven, dishwasher and a sink full of dirty dishes. The flies were big and loud, buzzing around the sink and colliding with a window that showed a messy yard out back. The rotting smell was worse in here, making me heave.

I went over to the sink, swatting at flies as they swarmed around me. Sitting among the dirty dishes, the carcass of a chicken crawled with maggots. They writhed over the flesh. I backed away.

The smell of rotting meat wasn't a zombie at all; it really was rotting meat. It looked like somebody had left here in a hurry. The back door was still slightly ajar. So the occupants had left the keys in the front door and fled out the back.

Remembering why I had entered the house, I wondered if they had taken their car with them. A quick search of the kitchen told me there were no car keys here. I went back to the hallway and closed the kitchen door to lessen the stink of the chicken.

In the living room, I found a key fob on the coffee table. I wondered if the people who lived here were still alive or if they were dead somewhere.

Either way, I was taking their car. A large bay window showed the street outside. Still deserted. I pointed the key fob at the row of cars and pressed the unlock button. The lights on a black Astra flashed.

If the car had fuel, I was out of here.

I checked the street again from the front door. All clear.

The Astra locked itself with a click by the time I reached it so I pressed the fob again and slid into the driver's seat. The car was fairly new and the inside was empty of clutter, unlike my own car, which was full of rock CDs in and out of their cases.

I started the engine and watched the lights on the fuel gauge climb to the three quarters full mark.

Breathing a sigh of relief, I put the car into first gear and pulled onto the road.

I drove along the coastal road, glancing out of the window at the sea below for any sign of *The Big Easy*, but she was nowhere to be seen. I could think about that later. Right now, I had to find a safe place away from the city.

Being in the car gave me more confidence. As long as I could avoid military checkpoints, I should be able to drive to a remote area and hide while I decided on my next move to get back to Lucy and our boat.

Despite the fact that the army had taken over the marina, the coastal road was free of any military presence.

I put my foot down a little and carefully picked up speed. I couldn't wait to see the back of the city but I had to make sure I didn't drive into a hidden checkpoint and get caught by soldiers.

Despite the shitty start to the day, my luck seemed to be changing and I drove out of the city without any problems. As I hit the road that wound between the green, misty mountains and the city was no longer in the rear-view mirror, I realised I had been breathing shallowly, almost holding my breath in anticipation of trouble.

I felt calmer now. Breathing more deeply, I cracked open the window to let some fresh air into the car.

I could not relax completely. There could be a military checkpoint anywhere on the road. I watched the road ahead carefully and kept the Astra at a steady 30 miles per hour.

The road wound inland and the sea disappeared from view, making me feel even more cut off from Lucy and *The Big Easy*. Trees and mountains blurred past the windows as

I drove farther away from the coast. I felt like I was abandoning Lucy but I had to find shelter, a hiding place. Besides, if she was on the boat, she was probably safe whereas I was in a shitload of danger.

I felt like a fish that had been washed up onshore and would suffocate unless it found its way back to the water. I had never been a fan of the sea before but now it was the only place I felt safe from the hell that had thrust itself upon the world.

I looked for side roads as I drove, the urge to get off the main road rising in my gut like boiling acid. If I stayed on this road for much longer, I would run into the army. They would put me in a Survivors Camp. Or they would kill me. Either way, I'd be dead. Better a quick bullet in the head than to get locked up like a sardine in a can, waiting for the zombies to arrive.

After half an hour of slow, tense driving, the mountains were replaced by woods. I saw a large wooden gate on the right and a dirt road that led beyond it into the trees. I pulled over, left the engine running, and got out to take a closer look.

The gate was held shut by a metal bolt but there were no locks. The road beyond disappeared into the trees. Maybe there was a house up there, a farm, or a herd of zombies. I had no idea. At least I would be off the main road. I slid the bolt back and swung the gate open.

After driving through, I closed it behind me and replaced the bolt. Getting back in the Astra quickly, I drove along the bumpy, narrow road, constantly checking the rear-view mirror and windows for trouble. The trees crowded close to the sides of the road and I half-expected a horde of the undead to come staggering out in front of me or crash through the trees and thrust their blue-skinned hands through the windows, clawing me with deadly nails.

Neither of those things happened. After a few minutes, the road took me out of the trees and through overgrown farmland inhabited by cows. A wooden sign nailed to a fencepost said "Mason's Farm".

The house was ahead, a two-storey stone building that looked deserted. There was a weather-worn wooden barn behind the house but no other buildings that I could see. No neighbours. The fields were bordered by trees and a wire fence on one side and mountains on the other. Remote. Isolated.

Perfect. If it was empty.

I stopped by the side of the house and sat in the car with the engine running. I lowered my window all the way and listened. Over the idling engine, all I could hear was birds in the trees and the breeze rustling through the grass. The air smelled of grass and manure and that was just fine.

I hit the button again and as the window whirred up, I picked up my baseball bat from the passenger seat.

I turned the engine off, got out, locked the car and pocketed the key. Standing there for a moment in the brightening morning sun, I listened again to my surroundings.

Nothing to indicate the presence of people or nasties. Seemed like it was just me, the cows, and the birds. Of course there could be a gang of killers waiting inside. They could be hiding behind the front door after seeing my approach along the dirt road.

Or it could be that when I opened the door, a wall of stench would hit me, followed by shambling undead.

Either way, I was opening the door. I didn't have too many options right now and I didn't want to go back to the main road.

I walked up to the brown wooden front door and knocked, gripping the bat tightly in my other hand. If there were people inside—living, friendly people—there was no harm in showing them I wasn't a bandit come to kill them. And I wasn't giving myself away by knocking; the house overlooked the dirt road and the Astra wasn't quiet.

No answer.

I listened, willing my senses to reach beyond the door into the house beyond but either the place was empty or my listening skills hadn't taken on superhuman powers.

Silence.

The door handle was made of brass, polished and worn from plenty of use over the years. I pulled it down.

The latch opened with a click and the door swung inwards.

I took a step back. I hadn't expected the place to be unlocked.

A gloomy hallway led into the house. There were pictures on the wall that looked like framed family photographs. The air smelled musty, as if the house had been closed up for a while, but there was no sickening taint of rotting flesh.

I stepped inside, bat held ready.

Nothing jumped out at me, no hands reached for me.

My heart was beating so loudly it felt like it was in my ears and I was sweating and shaking. I closed the front door.

From one of the framed photos, the Mason family looked down at me with smiles on their faces. Mr. and Mrs. Mason and two blonde girls aged around ten or twelve. The whole family was dressed in their best clothes for what looked like a professional photo session. I wondered how long ago that day was and where the Masons were now? Huddled together in a Survivors Camp or wandering out back infected with the virus?

I hoped it was the Survivors Camp and not only because it would be easier for me that way; they looked like a nice family. I hoped they'd made it.

Meanwhile, I was going to use their house for a short time.

A doorway to the left led to a living room with the usual furnishings: sofa, easy chairs and a TV. There was also a big stone fireplace, which would be useful.

I tried the light switch. The ceiling light came on.

Someone—probably the army—was keeping the infrastructure of the country running. I imagined soldiers would be posted at power stations and sewage plants, making sure we had electricity and water even as we became overrun with zombies. At least we would die with the basic amenities.

I turned off the light and went into the kitchen.

It was small and well-equipped like any farmhouse kitchen, I supposed. Not that farmhouse kitchens were my specialty subject; before the apocalypse I barely visited my own kitchen, preferring instead to order takeaway. I used my oven to reheat pizza or curry sometimes but that was about the extent of my cooking abilities beyond making toast.

The thought of food made me hungry. I decided to quickly check the rest of the house then find something to eat. There must be something edible in one of those cupboards.

The only other room downstairs was a utility room with a washer and dryer.

I went upstairs, past more family pictures, to the landing. Four doors. All closed.

I stood still for a moment and listened.

Nothing.

The first door was a double bedroom. The next two were the girls' rooms and the final door led to the bathroom. Toilet, bath, and a small walk-in shower.

I walked back along the hall, satisfied that the house was empty. The beds were all neatly made. I assumed the Mason family had followed the instructions on the Emergency Broadcast and left here to go to a Survivors Camp. There was no vehicle outside. They probably just packed a few essentials and drove to the nearest checkpoint, trusting their lives to the military and whatever government was running the country now.

Had Joe and my parents done the same? Handed their lives to the authorities with blind faith?

I went back downstairs to the kitchen. The cupboards were stocked with tins and dried food, including pasta and rice. There was a small green metal kettle on the gas hob and I found coffee and tea bags. No milk, of course, unless I tried milking one of the cows in the field, which I wasn't about to attempt, but other than that I could have a good meal here and take some supplies with me when I left.

I could plan my next move on a full stomach.

I reached for the kettle and picked it up to fill it.

I dropped it immediately, stepping back as it clattered to the floor.

The lid rolled away and steaming hot water spilled out over the floor tiles.

Hot water.

The kettle had recently boiled.

Someone was here.

Six

I CROUCHED LOW AND CREPT to the window. The house was empty but maybe someone was out there in the barn. They could have hidden there when they heard my car coming up the road. Were they afraid of me or were they waiting to ambush me? Maybe they had already disabled the Astra. Pulled the wires out of the engine or something.

The barn had a sliding door big enough to drive a tractor through. It was partly open. Beyond the door, there was darkness.

I wished Lucy were here. She was better at making decisions than I was, able to leap into action when the situation demanded it. Left to my own devices, I was too indecisive. Should I go out to the car, hope they hadn't touched it, and drive away? Or wait here until whoever was in the barn came out? What if they weren't in the barn at all and there was some part of the house I had missed?

I cast a glance over my shoulder at the hallway. I wished I had a key for the front door.

My legs were aching. I couldn't stay here, crouched behind the kitchen counter, for much longer.

The people in the barn—if they were in the barn—showed no intention of coming out. There could be a dozen people in there, all as crazy as the survivors I had encountered at the marina. I should get in the car and get out of here.

Decision made, I moved as quickly to the front door as I could while keeping low on my aching legs. Standing and shaking my legs to ease the pain, I prepared to open the door and run to the car. I dug the key fob out of my pocket. As soon as I opened the door, I would unlock the car and get into it before the potential killers in the barn knew what was happening.

I would find another house, one with fewer inhabitants.

I tried to calm my erratic breathing and counted myself down slowly.

3…

I placed my hand on the cool door handle.

2…

Tightened my grip on the handle and the baseball bat.

1…

I let out a low breath.

Go.

I pulled the door open and fled outside, fumbling for the "unlock" button on the key fob.

Something hit me in the stomach, forcing my breath out in an explosive *whoosh*. I barely had time to see the woman step out from her hiding place beside the door before she lashed at me with a fist. It connected squarely with my face and I saw a sudden shower of bright sparks in my vision.

I swung the bat blindly, felt her catch hold of it.

She wrenched it from my grasp and threw it into the grass.

Unarmed, I raised my fists, only too aware that I had never faced anyone in a fistfight and this was a bad time to start.

She stood in a fighter's stance, waiting for me to get closer like a praying mantis waiting for an insect to fly within reach of its spiked forelegs.

"I don't want to fight," I said, holding up my hands.

"Who the fuck are you?" She remained in her stance like a female Bruce Lee. The fact that she was Chinese added to the illusion. She wore a brown leather jacket over a black T-shirt and blue jeans over a black pair of boots. She was slim and tall with long raven hair and angry brown eyes.

"My name's Alex," I said. "I was just looking for somewhere to hide out for a while. I didn't know you were here. I'll leave." I almost added, "If you'll let me," but stopped myself.

She looked at me closely. "Are you alone? You drove here on your own but do you have friends around here? Hiding in the trees maybe?" She stared at the trees, her eyes searching for movement.

"No, I'm alone," I assured her.

She looked me over. "How have you survived this long?"

"I've been on a boat."

She nodded, as if that explained to her how someone like me could still be alive during a zombie apocalypse. She probably thought I had no chance on the mainland.

She was probably right.

Relaxing her fighter's stance, she said, "So what are you doing here? Where's your boat?"

I shrugged. "I don't know. I came ashore in the fog. I wanted to find a rowboat so we could get to shore more easily…"

"We?"

"I was with three friends when…the world went to shit. Two of them are dead. There's just Lucy and me left. We live on a boat. I shouldn't have left. I heard my brother on Survivor Radio and I wanted to see if I could find out anything so I needed a rowboat and…" I shrugged, feeling helpless. My stupid decisions were indefensible. "Lucy disappeared," I said, "and now I'm stuck."

She raised a quizzical eyebrow. "Why not just get another boat and go find her?"

"I was going to but the army are crawling all over the marina."

That caught her attention. "Really? Interesting."

"Can I leave now?" I asked.

"Where are you going to go? You said you have no clue where your boat is. You came here looking for shelter. You think you're going to find somewhere safer?"

"No, but…" I wasn't sure I wanted to stay there with a woman who punched first and asked questions later.

She laughed. "You can stay here when we're sure you are actually alone." She nodded to the dirt road where a tall, lanky guy in jeans and a Savatage tour T-shirt was walking towards the house. In one hand, he carried a tire iron. He saw the girl looking at him and gave her a thumbs-up.

She looked back at me. "You were telling the truth about being alone, anyway. I'm Tanya. The guy coming up the road is Sam. And the girl sitting on your car is Jax."

I turned to the Astra behind me. A pretty, young, petite woman with shoulder-length blonde hair sat cross-legged on the roof. She smiled, waved, and slid down to the ground. She wore a denim jacket and jeans and a white T-shirt. Her wooden baseball bat was propped against the car.

Sam got closer and Tanya said, "Everything okay?"

He nodded. "He's on his own. And he remembered to close the gate behind him." He was big and loose-limbed with short sandy hair and a soul patch.

"This is Alex," Tanya said.

"Hey, man." He raised a hand.

I nodded. I still wasn't sure if they were going to kill me. They knew I was here alone so why not? But they didn't seem like the killing types. They looked like they were ordinary people caught up in a deadly situation they had no control over, just like me.

"Give Jax your car keys and she'll put your car in the barn with ours," Tanya said. "We can't be too careful. The army might decide to come and take a look. I'd rather not advertise our presence."

I had dropped the key fob in my fight with Tanya. I picked it up and handed it to Jax. She took it and went over to the Astra, slid in and started the engine.

"You'd better come inside," Tanya said. "If you've been sailing along the coast, you might have some useful info."

And maybe they'd tell me what they were going to do with that info. They had a purposeful air about them, as if they had a mission beyond simple day-to-day survival.

Tanya and Sam went to the front door and I followed, aware of a dull ache across the bridge of my nose where Tanya had punched me.

She turned and said, "Aren't you forgetting something?"

I frowned, confused. "What do you mean?"

She pointed to the grass where my baseball bat lay. "Your bat. It's too dangerous to be unarmed." She grabbed a crowbar she had placed by the door.

I ran over and picked up my weapon. As I stood and turned back to the house, I felt a sudden panic in my gut.

Everything seemed too quiet. I closed my eyes and listened to the noises of Mason's Farm. I could hear my car being parked in the barn, the breeze on the grass and Tanya and Sam talking inside the house. I opened my eyes and shook my head. I was getting paranoid.

But as I reached the front door of the house, I realised my senses hadn't picked up a noise that didn't belong; they had detected that a sound was missing.

The birds in the trees had stopped singing.

Jax came running over from the barn. She ran past me and into the house. "We've got company!" she shouted.

All three of them came out of the front door and closed it behind them. "Get to the barn," Tanya told me. She sprinted to the barn with the others.

I followed and as I entered the barn, Sam slid the door closed behind me.

I felt trapped

Seven

THE BARN WAS SPACIOUS. THERE was a small tractor in there as well as my car and a white Jeep Cherokee I assumed belonged to Tanya. The barn smelled of hay and oil. Various farming implements stood against one wall and there were bales of hay piled in the corner beneath a wooden ladder that led to a hayloft. The others were climbing up the ladder. The barn was gloomy with the door closed but there was sunlight up in the loft so I assumed there must be a window. I followed them up the ladder.

The window was actually a window-sized opening in the wooden wall. A shutter that fit over the opening was open, allowing the sun to come into the loft and offering a perfect view of the house and the dirt road beyond.

Rucksacks and rolled up sleeping bags lay amongst the hay. Tanya, Jax and Sam were positioned around the window, peeking out at the house.

Tanya turned to glare at me. "If this is somebody you brought here, I will kill you, Alex."

"It isn't," I said. "I swear." I crawled over to the window. The farm looked deserted. "There's nobody out there," I whispered.

"Sshh!" Tanya held up a hand to silence me then pointed out of the window.

Coming up the dirt road was an olive green Land Rover. It halted twenty feet from the house and four soldiers poured out, taking up shooting stances to cover a 360-degree arc.

A fifth soldier climbed out of the passenger side of the vehicle and stood with hands on hips. He wore a maroon beret where the other soldiers wore helmets. He wore army trousers and boots but his top was a dark blue long-sleeved T-shirt that showed off his muscular physique. It was hard to see his face from this distance but I could see he had a moustache. He regarded the house and swept his eyes over the farm. I shrank back when his gaze fell on the barn but his inspection continued over the rest of the farm.

He pointed at the house and the four soldiers advanced to the front door in a tight line.

"Stand by," the man by the Land Rover said, then, "Go."

They kicked open the front door and went inside. I could hear shouts of "Clear!" as they entered each room.

"What if they check out the barn?" I whispered to nobody in particular.

"They will," Tanya replied.

"What do we do?" I asked.

"Fight or get captured."

"They have guns," I said. "We have bats and crowbars."

"If they capture you, you're dead anyway," Jax said, "so you might as well go down fighting."

"I know the Survivors Camps are bad," I said, "but…"

"Bad?" Tanya asked, incredulous. "You've been on that boat of yours for too long. You don't know what's really going on here, do you?"

"I…no," I admitted.

"I'll put this in simple terms," she said flatly. "If they take you to a Survivors Camp, you're as good as dead."

I thought of Joe and my parents.

"They're coming out," Jax said.

The four soldiers emerged from the house and took up positions at the Land Rover again. One of them spoke to the man in the maroon beret. He nodded and pointed at the barn.

The four soldiers got into their line and advanced across the dirt and grass towards us, assault rifles held steady.

"Fuck," Sam whispered.

"Everybody, get in the Jeep," Tanya whispered. She grabbed a backpack and ran over to the ladder and started down it. We all followed, Sam and Jax grabbing rucksacks and jostling for position in the line for the ladder. I ended up at the back. By the time I got down to ground level, the others were already in the vehicle. I got into the backseat with Sam. Tanya was in the driver's seat with Jax next to her on the passenger side.

Tanya hadn't started the Jeep. Her finger hovered over the Start button.

I felt helpless. The men outside were trained and they had guns. We had a Jeep Cherokee and baseball bats. If this was the end, my decision to come ashore in the fog had been the must stupid decision of my life. Lucy would never know what had happened to me and I would never know why she sailed away from the marina, leaving me on the mainland.

Outside the barn door, I heard the soldier's voice.

"Stand by."

A brief hesitation, then he spoke a simple word that sent my heart racing.

"Go."

Eight

THE DOOR SLID OPEN, LETTING in a shaft of light from outside. Four shadowy figures entered the barn, flanking the door. One of them shouted as Tanya started the Jeep and slammed it into first, sending the vehicle roaring forwards.

The soldiers had opened the door wide enough to allow themselves to slip into the barn so the gap wasn't large enough to get the Cherokee through. We hit the door with a crash of wood meeting metal. The door splintered and we drove through. Behind us, the soldiers started firing.

"Hold on," Tanya said through gritted teeth, pulling the wheel to the right and taking us into the field. I heard half a dozen bullets hit the rear of the Jeep with loud pinging sounds.

Tanya spun the wheel in the opposite direction and the Cherokee fishtailed before straightening up and speeding for the trees.

I risked a glance out of the back window. The soldiers were running for the Land Rover, their beret-headed commander gesturing at them angrily.

Tanya narrowly avoided two trees and we skidded onto the dirt road. She put her foot down and the Jeep picked up speed.

I pulled my seatbelt across my body and clicked it into the buckle. Everyone else did the same as we approached the wooden gate that led to the main road.

Behind us, the Land Rover gave chase. The man in the beret was shouting into a radio.

"There might be more of them on the road," I told Tanya. "He's talking to someone on the radio."

She nodded and said, "Hold tight."

We went through the gate with a loud bang and as Tanya spun the wheel to straighten us up on the road, I saw the gate lying in pieces. The Land Rover was closer now, almost at the remains of the gate.

Tanya floored the accelerator and we sped along the road.

Jax opened the glove compartment and took out a map. She unfolded it and ran her finger along the roads. "There's a left turn ahead," she said. "A side road that leads north."

Tanya nodded, watching the road ahead closely. "You've got to be kidding me," she muttered.

I leaned forward to see what she had seen.

A herd of zombies stood on the road, most of them wandering aimlessly, some of them staggering towards us. There must have been a hundred of them. They were standing on the road and trudging between the trees at either side. There was no way around them.

"Go through them," Sam suggested. He glanced out of the back window. "The soldiers are getting closer. We have to go through them."

Tanya nodded grimly but slowed our speed slightly. "This is going to get messy."

We hit them with a heavy thud and I saw two of them go down immediately. The others crowded towards the Cherokee, their arms outstretched as they reached for us. Their yellow eyes held a look of malevolence. They moaned as their searching hands found the glass of the windows, the steel of the doors, and not yielding flesh.

More thuds came from the front of the vehicle as we drove through the herd. The zombies closed in around us like a sea of rotting blue flesh. Tanya was forced to slow down. She gunned the engine in frustration and we made slow progress through the mass of rotting bodies.

I looked out of the back window. The Land Rover had stopped a safe distance from the nasties. The soldiers weren't following us into the throng of hungry undead. But the man in the beret was climbing out and going around the back. He disappeared for a few seconds behind the Land Rover then reappeared and went down on one knee.

"He's got a rocket launcher!" Sam said.

"Still think the army is our friend?" Tanya asked, glancing at me over her shoulder. "We need to get out of here…now!"

She put her foot down and we roared forwards through the mass of zombies. The increased speed and impact of the bodies brought us to a sudden halt. Tanya gunned the engine. "We're stuck. There're too many of them under the wheels." The front of the Cherokee had lifted into the air, supported by a pile of bodies underneath the chassis.

"We need to get out," Jax said, looking back at the soldier with the rocket launcher, "or we're going to get fried."

We still weren't clear of the herd. While the other three grabbed their rucksacks and opened their doors, I hesitated, my trembling hand on the door handle. There was no choice. If I stayed in the vehicle, I would be toast.

I opened the door with as much force as I could, sending a zombie staggering backwards, and came out swinging my bat wildly. The sound of the wood thwacking into zombie heads was sickening. The stench of rotted flesh was overpowering. The sound of the nasties' hungry moans made the hairs on my arms and neck stand on end.

I concentrated on the stretch of clear road past the herd. I swung at anything that came near me. The zombies at the rear of the Jeep realised their prey was out of the vehicle, exposed and vulnerable, and tried to crowd closer to us, jostling with each other in their eagerness to tear into our flesh with teeth and nails.

I swung the bat wildly, trying to clear a path to that sweet patch of clear road ahead. For every zombie I knocked over, another replaced it instantly.

At one point, I felt a hand rake down my back and I thought I had been scratched, infected, but the nasty's nails didn't penetrate my hoodie. I was lucky but I knew my luck wouldn't hold out much longer. There were too many of them.

The road ahead might as well be a thousand miles away.

I tripped over a body and went down hard, feeling a flare of pain in my shoulder as it hit the hard road.

A dozen blue-skinned monsters stood above me, ready to tear into the video-gaming geek who was lucky to have lived this long in the zombie apocalypse.

Then everything became light, sound and heat. A light so bright it burned my eyes, a sound so loud it deafened me, and a heat so intense it seared my skin.

Nine

I ROLLED ONTO MY STOMACH, feeling the rough road beneath my fingers. The only sound I could hear was a constant whine in my head. My ears felt like they had been stuffed with wool. My skin felt tender, like I had been burned by the sun. I staggered to my feet unsteadily. The Cherokee was a flaming tangle of white metal and broken glass. Angry flames and black smoke plumed from the remains of the roof.

The zombies around me had been destroyed by the blast. They lay on the road like blue-skinned rag dolls. There was a stench of cooking meat in the air and I gagged, trying not to be sick. I didn't have time to be sick. Most of the herd, the nasties that had been far enough away from the Cherokee, were still "alive". They shambled towards me.

STORM

A hand grabbed my shoulder from behind and I whirled, bat ready. It was Jax. Black dirt smeared her face but she looked otherwise intact. She said something to me but I couldn't hear anything over the whine. She pulled me off the road and into the trees. Tanya and Sam were waiting for us there.

We ran.

After a few minutes, I was out of breath. The whine in my head was still there but now I could hear other sounds as well, muffled but definitely there. Tanya and Sam speaking. The crunch of twigs beneath our boots. My own laboured breathing and the sound of my rapid heartbeat.

I slowed to a stumbling pace and let them get ahead of me. There was no way I could keep up. Story of my life. Always lagging behind everyone else. My stumbling jog slowed to a walk. I could barely breathe, never mind run. At least my hearing was improving with each passing minute. The whine had faded into a dull background noise.

I made my way through the forest at my own pace, unable to do anything else, and was surprised when I found Tanya, Jax and Sam waiting for me.

"You okay?" Jax asked as I reached them.

I nodded. "I can't…move very fast."

"We'll take a breather here," Tanya said. She sat down on a fallen log.

I did the same, sitting on the ground and leaning back against a tree trunk. "What are your stories?" I asked. "You all seem to know how to handle yourselves."

"We've been in some tricky situations before all this shit went down," Tanya said. "I was a reporter for the BBC. Sam was my cameraman. We've been to the Middle East a few times, reported on the war. We made a documentary on the US and British forces in Iraq. Sam was also the cameraman for Vigo Johnson."

"The survival guy?" Vigo Johnson made TV shows about how to survive in various situations.

"Yeah," Sam said. "We went all over the world and got into some tough situations. A lot of people think all that stuff is faked for TV but it was real. Usually just me and him stuck up a mountain in the middle of nowhere or deep in a tropical jungle. I filmed a lot of it on a handheld camera. Whatever Vigo did, I did too. But the viewers rarely saw me on their screens."

"What about you?" I asked Jax.

"I'm a journalist," she said. "We were making a documentary when the shit hit the fan and the army started taking people to the camps. We went on the run. There were seven of us to begin with. Now, only we three are left."

I nodded. These people had seen death and misery just like everyone else.

"We should get moving," Tanya said.

I stood up, feeling only slightly refreshed after the short break, and we started through the forest again. I wondered what Lucy was doing. Was she sailing up and down the coast looking for me? Did she think I was dead? How long would she stay in the area before she forgot about me and moved on? Where would she go? Where were my three new companions going?

I caught up with Jax. "Do you guys have a plan?"

She nodded. "Of course. Find somewhere safe to stay. Eat and drink before moving on tomorrow."

"I meant a long-term plan. Are you moving on to anywhere in particular?"

She looked at me as if deciding whether or not she could trust me. "Yeah. Somewhere particular."

"Where's that?" I asked, trying to sound nonchalant. It seemed like their destination was a closely-guarded secret or something.

"Cornwall," she said.

I nodded as if I understood why they would want to go there. "Good choice," I said. "Not as populated as the rest of the country. Plenty of remote areas to hide."

"Yeah," she said noncommittally. I had hoped to draw more information out of her but my social skills were seriously lacking. Did they know something about Cornwall? It had remote areas, as I had said, but there were more remote places in Scotland so why not head north across the border? What was it about Cornwall that was drawing them there?

"Any other reason?" I asked Jax.

"Maybe," she said.

This line of questioning was getting me nowhere. I should just keep my mouth shut and concentrate on how I was going to find Lucy and *The Big Easy* again.

Trouble was, I had no ideas at all.

After a few more minutes of relentless trudging through the woods, I asked her, "Why are the army trying to kill us?"

She looked at me like I had just asked her why the sky was blue. "You really don't know, do you?"

I shook my head. "I thought they were supposed to be protecting people from the zombies, not trying to kill civilians."

She laughed. "They do what the government order them to do. It isn't about protection; it's about control. Even now, after the entire country has gone to hell, the politicians spread lies and try to control the people."

"Lies? I don't understand."

"Tell me what you know about the virus outbreak, Alex."

"Okay," I said, "it comes from India. There was a doctor quarantined in a hospital in London. It spread from there." I remembered the news reports I had read on board the *Solstice*. "And it's infected America. Probably the rest of the world too."

She shook her head. "All lies fed to you by the media. That's why we're going to Cornwall. We're going to tell everybody what's really happening."

Ten

I HAD NO IDEA WHAT Jax meant by that and I had no time to ask. Tanya and Sam suddenly dropped to crouching positions and gestured at us to do the same. We complied and crawled up to where they crouched peering through the trees.

The forest dipped down to a road ahead. It was more a track than a road and it looked like it had been made by tractors. Twin grooves had been gouged into the mud by big tires and between the grooves grew a line of grass. I looked up along the track and spotted a red painted metal gate. Beyond the gate was a muddy field and in the distance I could see a low wooden barn. I assumed there was a house up there somewhere but the trees cut off my line of sight.

"Looks like a farm," Sam whispered. "We should check it out."

"Do we really want to?" I asked. "We didn't do so well at the last farm."

"This one looks more remote," Tanya said. "There's no road, only that muddy track. Jax, have you got the map?"

Jax took the map from her backpack and unfolded a portion of it. She located our position and the farm. "It's a few miles to the main road," she said. "We should take a closer look."

Tanya nodded and set off down the slope. We followed until we all stood on the muddy track. I glanced back along the track. It disappeared around a bend in the distance. In front of us, it ran up to the gate and disappeared into the field. The gate was held shut with a short blue cord that was looped over the metal gate post.

We could see the farmhouse now. It sat waiting for us just beyond the barn. There were no signs of life.

Tanya opened the gate and said, "Come on."

We trudged through the mud towards the house.

"I hope there's food in there," I said. It was lunchtime and my stomach was growling at how empty it was.

"Don't worry, man, we'll find something," Sam said. "And if we don't, there are some granola bars in my backpack."

I wasn't sure a granola bar was going to sustain me for the rest of the day. I felt exhausted from all the fighting, running, and nearly getting blown up by a rocket launcher. I needed something substantial in my belly.

The farmhouse was a two-storey stone structure like the Mason's house. But unlike the Mason place, this one had a garage with a white metal door attached to the house and a wooden porch that looked like it had once been painted white but was so weathered that the paint had flaked away, revealing faded wood beneath. Only a few stubborn lines of paint remained.

Sam went up onto the porch and tried the door. "Locked." He went to the window, cupped his hands around his eyes and pressed his face to the glass. He stepped back. "Wow, freaky."

"What is it?" Tanya asked.

"There's an old woman in there. She's turned but she's sitting calmly on the sofa like she's watching the TV."

Tanya nodded. "That's what happens when they turn but there's no stimulus. They replicate old behaviours. I bet the entire family has gone nasty and they're all locked in there."

"We should move on," I suggested. I'd had enough of zombie-killing for one day.

"No, we go in and clear the place," Tanya said. "We don't have many options. I don't want to be outside at night when it's harder to see the zombies coming. This place shouldn't be too hard to clear. Just a family in there."

I nodded. I didn't much like the idea of going in there and killing a family, even if they were zombified, but I liked the idea of sleeping outside even less.

Sam went back to the front door and kicked it with the sole of his boot, putting all his weight behind it. He was a big guy and the wooden door cracked slightly but stayed shut. He kicked it a second time and it gave, opening with a crash. "Knock, knock," Sam said, brandishing his tire iron as he went inside.

The girls followed and I took up the rear, hoping that by the time I got inside, the killing would be done. But as I entered, Tanya said, "Alex, take the upstairs." She and Jax were moving through the downstairs rooms. Sam was in the living room, disposing of the TV-watching old lady zombie.

I went upstairs quickly, wanting to get it over and done with. As I reached the landing, the smell of decaying meat hit me. There were four doors up here. Two were open. One of them was the bathroom and the other a bedroom out of which a zombie staggered, arms outstretched. He wore a flannel shirt and jeans and looked like he had been in his fifties. I brought the bat back with both hands and swung it as hard as I could at his head. He went down like a sack of rotted potatoes and lay on the carpet unmoving.

I checked the bedroom he had come out of for further inhabitants but it was empty. A patch of dried blood and gore on the sheets told me the nasty had lain there for a long while. Zombies didn't sleep as far as I knew so he was probably going through the motions of his former life, as Tanya had said.

I went to the first closed door and opened it. The room was empty. Rock band posters on the walls and a game console attached to a large TV in the corner told me it probably belonged to a teenager. There was no sign of him in the room. Maybe he had been away at college when the virus outbreak started.

The next room was also empty. The light floral wallpaper and knitting on the chair in the corner probably meant it belonged to the old lady downstairs. Whatever she had been knitting would never be finished now.

I went downstairs to find the others.

Sam was outside, dragging the old lady's rotting body across the mud. I found Tanya and Jax in the kitchen.

"Did you find any more?" I asked them.

"No," Jax said, shaking her head.

"There's one upstairs," I said. "Looks like the farmer."

"The old lady was probably his mother," Tanya said. "No wife? Kids?"

"There's a teenager's bedroom upstairs. Maybe their son was away at the time and never came home."

She walked lithely into the hallway and pointed at a photograph on the wall. It showed a man in his fifties with a pretty blonde woman and a dark-haired boy of sixteen or seventeen. They were all smiling at the camera. "So where's the woman?" Tanya asked.

"Maybe she was away too. Visiting the son in college or something." I didn't really care where the wife was as long as she wasn't here trying to tear my throat out. Tanya and Jax were journalists so I supposed they had more curiosity about these things than I did.

Tanya went back into the kitchen and opened a door that led into a large pantry. There was plenty of food in there and my stomach did a little flip of anticipation. Tanya wasn't searching for food, though. She checked the dining room before going out into the hallway and opening a small door underneath the stairs.

"There's a basement," she said, pointing to an opening in the floor and a ladder leading down into darkness.

Tanya leaned over the opening and tried to see what was down there. "Too dark," she said.

Remembering the working lights at Mason's Farm, I reached in and found a switch on the wall. I clicked it on and the area beneath the stairs and the basement below lit up. Tanya went down the ladder cautiously. A moment later, she called, "It's okay. Come down."

Jax went down and I followed. When we reached the tiny basement, I had to stoop to keep from hitting my head on the low ceiling. The basement was actually little more than a crawl space used for storing tools and sports equipment, which I guessed had belonged to the son.

The wife was in the corner, recognisable as the woman in the photo upstairs by her blonde hair. She was dead. Really dead. Not turned.

"She must have come down here when her husband and the old lady changed," I said. "She was too scared to go back up into the house and eventually she just died down here. She didn't even dare put the light on."

"It doesn't make sense," Tanya said. "There are things down here she could have used as weapons. She could have gotten out of the house. Why stay down here waiting to die when you can fight your way out?"

"Not everybody thinks the same way," I said. "Where would she go to if she got out? Her husband had turned. The old lady might have been her mother. She probably thought everyone in the world had changed like them. She had nothing to live for."

"What about the son?" Tanya didn't seem to understand the concept of giving up, not fighting for survival.

I shrugged. "She must have thought he was changed or dead. And if he was alive, how would she find him? She wouldn't last five minutes out there."

Tanya nodded slowly. I could see she was trying to understand but her job took her to places where situations were dire yet people fought for survival. It was what she knew.

If I hadn't been with Mike, Elena, and Lucy when the shit hit the fan, I probably would have ended up like this woman. Afraid to leave my house. Somebody would find me one day and I would be lying dead among video games and fast food containers.

"We need to give her a proper burial," Jax said.

Tanya nodded. "I can't believe she didn't fight."

I didn't say anything else but as I looked down on the corpse of the woman, I totally understood her choice. Fight for what? She had no future.

And now that I was separated from Lucy, what was I fighting for? A life of roaming from one farm to the next, trying to stay one step ahead of the army and clearing houses of zombies? That was no life.

Being with Mike, Elena, and Lucy had taught me that sometimes I had to fight for what I wanted.

I was willing to fight to get back to Lucy. That was the only thought keeping me going right now.

Without that thin strand of hope, I might as well be like the dead woman lying at my feet.

Eleven

WE REMOVED THE FARMER'S BODY and dumped it next to the old lady's in a ditch. Sam and I found shovels in the basement and dug a grave behind the house for the blonde woman. For some reason, we afforded her more respect because she had died without becoming one of the nasties.

When I thought about it logically, it didn't make sense that we should treat the zombies any differently; they had died too. But the virus turned them into monsters and that threw all logic out of the window.

They died as monsters and we treated them as such.

After we buried the woman, Sam and I stood over the fresh grave silently for a moment. We bowed our heads. I thought about the friends I had lost in the apocalypse and I hoped I didn't lose any more. I wasn't religious in any way but I said a silent prayer that I would find Lucy and she would be alive and well.

Sam raised his head and looked at me. There were tears in his eyes. He had been thinking about his own loved ones. "Let's go back inside, man. We've done all we can for this woman."

I nodded and as we walked to the house I wondered if these three people now numbered among my friends. I barely knew them but they seemed like decent people. They had let me join them and we had fought together. I didn't know how long they would let me stay with them…they seemed to have some mission to carry out…and I didn't know what I would do when we parted ways but for now I was glad to be with them.

As we reached the door, Sam turned to me with a serious look on his face. "There's something we need to do now, Alex. It's very important."

"What's that?" I asked.

A grin spread across his face. "We need to find beer."

*

Later, Jax and I sat in the living room while Tanya and Sam fussed about in the kitchen cooking a meal. They had a friendly, joking banter between them and I wondered if they were a couple, or should be a couple. Outside, it was getting dark. We had opened all the windows in the house and left them open all afternoon to let fresh air into the house. The rotting smell was gone and now the house was filled with the fragrance of chicken being fried in herbs and spices. In his search for beer, Sam had found a freezer packed with meat.

He had also eventually found a case of beer in the pantry. A dozen bottles of Spitfire ale. A half-drained bottle sat in front of me on the coffee table as I waited for the meal. The smell of the chicken was driving me crazy.

Jax had lit a fire in the stone fireplace. The logs crackled and popped. With the ceiling light dimmed, the fire flickered orange on the walls, making the room seem cozy. Jax had unfolded her map and laid it on the rug in front of the fireplace. It showed the surrounding area and Swansea to the west. She had placed a second map next to it. That was a map of Britain, showing the contours of the coast.

I had asked her earlier about the "media lies" she had mentioned in the forest and she said they would explain everything to me after we ate. I couldn't argue with that; right now, food was my main priority.

Sam stuck his head through the door. "Come and get it."

We gathered in the dining room around a large oak table. Sam and Tanya had set out plates and cutlery and in the middle of the table sat two big serving bowls. One was full of boiled white rice. The other contained a mouth-watering chicken curry. Four bottles of Spitfire sat next to the rice.

I sat and said, "That looks and smells great."

Sam laughed and said, "Tanya's curries are great but she makes them spicy, man. If you're not used to them, they go right through you." He looked at Tanya and said, "We'll probably be fighting zombies tomorrow and Alex will have to excuse himself to go shit behind a tree."

She slapped him on the shoulder playfully. "I'm not taking the blame for that. You had just as much a hand in making it as I did. You're the one who was heavy-handed with the spices."

"I had to do something to cover up the way you fried the chicken with too much coriander," he said, looking at me and winking, letting me in on his joke.

"You liar!" Tanya said.

"Well it smells great," I said. We set about loading the curry and rice onto our plates and grabbing a bottle of beer each.

"Who's going to do the toast?" Jax asked.

"I'll do it," Sam said. He raised his bottle and said, "The fallen and the lost."

We all repeated it and started eating. The curry tasted amazing, despite Sam's jokes.

"How about a little radio?" Sam asked through a mouthful of food. He went out of the room and I heard him digging about in his backpack. He came back in with a small digital radio and placed it in the middle of the table. He switched it on and the familiar, smooth voice of DJ Johnny Drake filled the room.

"…to all the survivors out there alone. This one is for you from Matt in Survivors Camp Delta. This is The

Doors and 'Riders on the Storm'." The music started and we listened to it as we ate. Sam sang along here and there but mainly we just let it work its magic on us. In this post-apocalyptic world, music had gained an added importance beyond its ability to lift our moods; it was a relic of the old world.

Unlike other relics such as cars and fast food restaurants and coffee shops, music seemed alive. It spoke to a deep place inside us. It was the same with books. I had read a selection of books on *The Big Easy* and my mind craved more. Even though the books on the boat were thriller novels that I might not have read before the apocalypse—I usually stuck to sci fi and horror—they nourished my soul by giving me a connection with the past that other inanimate objects could not.

As soon as the radio had been turned on, the mood in the dining room went up. I felt easy, relaxed. The beer helped but mainly it was Jim Morrison singing about life, and the mellow keyboards. When The Doors finished, the Eurythmics song "Here Comes the Rain Again" started. Over the opening bars, Johnny Drake said, "This is a request for Lisa in Survivors Camp Gamma."

"They're naming the camps now," Jax said.

Tanya nodded.

As we finished the meal, I wondered how many times the farmer and his family had sat around this table enjoying dinner together. They could not have guessed that one day the world would be changed forever, they would all be dead, and a group of strangers would be sitting at the table listening to music and eating curry. For that family, it was all over.

Maybe they were the lucky ones.

We pushed the empty plates away and took our beers into the living room where the fire still crackled in the fireplace. Sam brought the radio in and placed it on the mantelpiece. Rhiannon was singing about an umbrella.

"Come and look at this map," Tanya said, pointing to the map of Britain. I sat on the rug next to her.

"Is it possible to take a boat from here"—she indicated the coast near our current location— "to here?" She pointed farther south at the city of Truro in Cornwall.

I had been to Cornwall on holiday when I was ten years old. My parents had taken Joe and me to Truro to look at the port. There had been some big ships there. "Yes, it's possible to take a boat there," I said, "but why Truro? It's no different from any other city."

"It is different," Tanya replied, "because that's where the radio station is being broadcast from." She looked at me closely but I didn't get her point.

I looked at Jax and Sam sitting on the sofa. "I don't understand."

Jax leaned forwards and told me their plan.

"We're going to take over Survivor Radio."

Twelve

"I STILL DON'T UNDERSTAND," I said. "Why?"

"We're only going to take it over temporarily," Tanya said. "We need to get a message out to anyone who's listening."

"What message?"

"The people in the Survivors Camps need to leave. The people outside of the camps need to stay there and not report to the military checkpoints."

I looked from one to the other of my new friends. The firelight flickered on their solemn faces. They were serious. They were actually considering taking over Survivor Radio. I could only imagine how well the army must be guarding their one media channel. How did Tanya, Jax, and Sam think they were going to get into the studio? Just walk in under the noses of the soldiers?

"I've seen what happens in those camps," I said. "I'm sure the people in them already know they should leave."

"They're being fed misinformation," Jax said. "As far as they know, there isn't anywhere safe to go. They're like that woman in the basement...afraid to leave because they don't think there's safety anywhere else."

"There isn't," I reminded her.

"Yes, there is," Tanya said. "Just not in this country."

"Where?"

"America."

I shook my head, remembering the news reports I had seen on the *Solstice*. "The virus has reached America. They're as infected as we are."

"That's not true," Jax said.

Maybe they just didn't know it yet, hadn't seen the news reports on the internet. "It was on the internet news. I saw the reports with my own eyes. The president called a state of emergency. One of the headlines said there was a virus outbreak in the U.S."

"When was this?"

I tried to count off the days in my mind. "Six or seven days ago."

Sam laughed and shook his head. "That was propaganda bullshit, man."

"You can't know that."

"Yeah, I can. Vigo Johnson is in the States right now. I spoke to him on a satellite phone two days ago. All they knew over there for a while was that Britain had gone dark. The U.S. government sent military aircraft over and looked at images from spy satellites and now they have some idea of what is happening but there's no virus over there. It's only here."

"What about India?" I asked, "That's where the virus came from."

Jax shook her head. "No, Alex, that's a lie. The news reports said there was a patient zero in London but I had been investigating reports of an unknown virus a week before that story came out. There were sightings of patients turning blue and staggering out of hospitals before the London story was concocted.

"These sightings and reports started in Scotland and moved south across the country. They didn't originate in London. The government is trying to wash their hands of all responsibility by blaming a virus from another country. The truth is, the thing started in Scotland. Probably escaped from a military test centre or something. My bet is it all started on Apocalypse Island."

"Apocalypse Island?" I wondered if these people were journalists for respected media outlets or conspiracy theory websites.

"It's a nickname," Jax said, "for a government facility on an island off the coast of Scotland. The place is run by scientists conducting experiments into diseases like foot and mouth and mad cow disease. If this virus came from that area, it must be from Apocalypse Island. Somebody messed up and it got to the mainland. The rest was inevitable once it reached a population of people to infect."

"Have you seen this island?" I asked.

She shook her head. "But we've all heard about it. And if it's true, that's where the virus came from."

I took a deep swallow of beer as I tried to process what I was being told. "Does it matter where the virus came from? The fact is, it's here. I know you guys are journalists and want to get to the bottom of things like this but for people like me, all that matters is that there are zombies trying to kill us."

"It matters, Alex," Tanya said, "because if they created this virus, they might have a vaccine. Something that stops you from turning if you get bit. Don't you think the people have a right to know if that's the case?"

"If there's a vaccine, they'd be injecting everyone in the camps," I suggested.

"And what happens then, man?" Sam asked. "Everyone wouldn't feel so helpless. They might leave the "safety" of the camps and find out that the rest of the world is hunky dory. Everyone would flee by any means possible, leaving the politicians in control of nothing but a country full of the undead. The way things are now, they are still in control of the people. That's what they want.

"They can't have it any other way. If the rest of the world found out the truth and it was a manmade virus that escaped from a government facility, the people in charge would be mass murderers. They would be tried as such. No way, man…better to spread propaganda and keep the population under control."

I wasn't sure how much of this I believed. I had never trusted the media. Tanya, Jax, and Sam worked for an industry that was known for putting a spin on everything. On the other hand, I had seen with my own eyes the military takeover of the marina at Swansea. The story would explain that. There might be a grain of truth in what they were telling me but they were filling in the rest themselves.

But their plan to take over Survivor Radio had me interested. Lucy listened to Survivor Radio. Maybe I could get a message to her. And Johnny Drake was playing requests for people in the Survivors Camps, which meant he had some form of communication with those camps. I might be able to get a message to Joe or find out where he and my family were.

The rest of it…Apocalypse Island, the government lies…didn't concern me. But if the story I had just heard was true and the rest of the world was uninfected, I could find Joe and my parents, rendezvous with Lucy and sail for America on *The Big Easy*. We could escape this hell.

All I had to do was help Tanya, Jax, and Sam break into a radio station in Cornwall and take over the government-controlled broadcast for long enough to get a message out. Then escape with my life.

Easy.

Yeah, right.

But what other option did I have? This was a chance to contact Lucy. The only chance I would ever have.

I looked at Tanya and nodded. "We'll need to get a boat. Swansea marina is out."

"Every other marina will be exactly the same," she said. "They're controlling every way into and out of the country."

"So what do we do?"

"We have to steal a boat from under their noses."

Thirteen

THE NEXT MORNING, I AWOKE on the sofa as sunlight streamed in through the window. I had found fresh sheets and a pillow in the linen closet and used them to make my night on the sofa more comfortable, but when I moved, I felt a painful stiffness in all my joints and muscles.

Tanya, Jax, and Sam had taken their sleeping bags upstairs to spend the night on the bedroom floors. Nobody wanted to sleep in the beds of the dead old lady or farmer. Sam had taken the teenage son's room and I could hear him snoring up there.

I rolled off the sofa onto the floor and spent several painful minutes getting to my feet before staggering to the window. It was sunny but there were dark clouds over the trees. A good day to steal a boat from a military-occupied marina? Was there ever a good day for that?

I went upstairs to the bathroom and checked myself in the mirror after taking off my "Sail To Your Destiny" T-shirt. My chest and back were covered in ugly purple bruises. The bridge of my nose was swollen where Tanya had punched me. The skin on my arms and face had blistered from the heat of the exploding Jeep Cherokee.

I looked a mess.

Even more of a mess than usual.

How much longer was I going to survive? And even if I did stay alive, would I remain mentally stable or would I become like the feral survivors I had fought at the marina?

I remembered the man I had killed on the beach. Best not to think about that; it was one of the thoughts that could send me spiraling into depression.

I removed the rest of my clothes and took a shower, using the shampoo and citrus-scented gel in there. The hot water stung my bruised and blistered skin but I stood under the spray for as long as I could, letting it wash over me and wash away the dirt and grime that I felt was ingrained in my flesh.

By the time I was dressed again, the others were in the kitchen searching for breakfast. Jax was in the pantry tossing tins of food out to Sam. He caught them and lined them up on the counter, inspecting the labels. Tanya was boiling the kettle, making coffee for everyone. I was glad to see four mugs. I needed caffeine. The plan we had formulated to get a boat from the marina was a crazy one. I needed to be alert.

"Hey, dude, you want baked beans or tinned tomatoes for breakfast?" Sam indicated the tins with a flourish.

"I'll take beans."

He handed a tin of beans to me. "There're saucepans hanging up over there if you want to heat them up."

"Cold is fine." I found the cutlery drawer and fished out a fork. As I leaned against the wall and ate, Tanya brought me a mug of steaming black coffee.

"You okay with today's plan?" she asked me.

"I understand it," I said, "but I don't know if I'm okay with it."

She grinned. "You'll be fine. Just think, we could all be safe on a boat later today."

"A boat headed to a city that is probably heavily guarded, not to mention full of zombies. I looked at the map last night. We have to sail up the River Fal, then the Truro River to get to Truro Harbour. If there are army positions along those rivers, we'll be sitting ducks."

"You worry too much, Alex."

"We also have to sail past Falmouth Harbour to get onto the river. The army presence there is going to be a lot stronger than at the Swansea marina; Falmouth Harbour is much bigger."

"So we'll wait until night time and sneak past them under cover of darkness."

"It won't be that easy."

"Then we'll improvise. How long will it take us to get to the mouth of the river?"

I shrugged. "Maybe two or three days. We have to go south from here, sail around Land's End then head north along the East Coast until we get to Falmouth. I don't know anything about navigation and I suggest we take it slow and easy." I thought, but didn't add, that there was no sense rushing into danger.

"Fine. No worries." She took her coffee and went into the living room.

She might not be worried, but I was. The more I thought about taking a boat up the river, the more nervous I became. We could be blown out of the water with nowhere to run. That was if we even managed to get a boat in the first place. I had my doubts that the plan we had formulated the previous night was going to work; there were too many variables, too many chances for something to go wrong.

This trip was my only chance to get a message to Lucy, otherwise I wouldn't even be considering it. I forced myself to finish the cold beans, despite a sudden loss of appetite. I would need the energy later.

We finished breakfast in silence. I was thinking about the task ahead and guessed the others were too. Sam had discovered a green Citroen in the garage last night but the vehicle we were most interested in was the farmer's dark blue Land Rover Defender parked behind the house. The keys had been hanging on a hook by the back door.

After formulating our plan, we had checked the fuel gauge on the Defender. The tank held enough petrol for what we had in mind.

We all piled in. I got in the back with Sam while Tanya took the wheel and Jax sat beside her, map spread out on her lap.

We drove down to the gate and I jumped out to open it and let the Land Rover through. I re-closed the gate, jumped back in, and we set off down the muddy track to the main road.

"This is where we saw the herd," Jax said, pointing to an area on the map, "and this is where we are now. If we take a left on the main road and the first left after that, we should be in the general vicinity. They might have moved but unless something caught their attention, they're more likely to just wander around the same area for a while."

Tanya nodded. "How far is it to the marina from there?"

Jax pointed at the map. "The marina's here."

"Okay," Tanya said, "let's go and collect some zombies."

Dark clouds filled the sky. I hoped they weren't an omen of bad luck.

Or something worse.

Fourteen

WHEN WE REACHED THE AREA where we had seen the herd of zombies the day before, the first thing I noticed was a smell of burnt flesh. Even with the Land Rover's windows closed, the stench was strong.

"Jesus, Alex, you could have waited," Sam joked, elbowing me lightly. I wondered if his attempt at humour covered a deeper fear of what we were about to attempt.

Ahead of us, the Jeep Cherokee lay on its side, a black burned-out shell of metal. Around it was the charred remains of dead zombies. In the shadows beneath the trees on each side of the road, the rest of the herd stood staring at us with malevolent yellow eyes. They shambled towards us, letting out a collective moan of hunger, rage, or whatever it was they felt when they saw living people.

The herd had thinned but there were still enough of them for what we had in mind. When they reached the road and staggered closer to us, Tanya moved the Defender forwards slowly.

The zombies followed.

As we set off down the road with the undead shambling along behind, I wondered if our plan had a hope in hell of succeeding. We were going to lead the herd to the marina and create enough of a distraction to allow us to sneak into the marina shop and grab a set of boat keys.

The keys to the marina's hire boats were kept beneath the counter in the shop and numbered. Our plan was to grab a few sets of keys, find the correspondingly-numbered boats and take the one that was moored farthest out along the jetty to allow a faster escape.

The plan sucked in so many ways.

We were going to ditch the Land Rover before we got to the marina to make ourselves less conspicuous. That meant we would be exposed on foot between an army unit and a herd of zombies.

For all we knew, the army might have taken the hire boat keys from the marina shop. Then we would be trapped with no boat and no vehicle.

Even if we managed to get a key, the boat we chose could be out of fuel. That was doubtful since they were hire boats and therefore likely to be topped up but it was a possibility.

Then, even if we got out to sea in a fuelled boat, we could easily be shot out of the water. I had seen a tank at the marina and the army probably had mortars set up there too. We could execute the plan perfectly only to be blown up as we got out on the waves.

I told myself to stop being so pessimistic. It wasn't like I had any other options. This plan had to work.

I wished I was at sea now, safe in a boat, away from the shambling hordes of undead.

They followed us along the road with hate burning in their yellow eyes. I wondered how aware they were. Did they have memories of their old lives? Or were their thoughts long gone, their bodies mindlessly reacting to stimuli in an attempt to spread the virus? The hateful glares made me think that there were some remnants of intelligence left in those rotting skulls, along with simple, dark emotions.

I counted at least fifty of them lurching along behind us. More than enough to create chaos once we reached the marina.

Sam looked at the rotting, walking dead and shook his head slowly. "They were once people like us, man. Now look at them. Monsters. This is why we have to tell everybody the truth about where the virus came from. Someone has to pay for causing this."

My own motives weren't anywhere near as noble as Sam's. I just wanted to find Lucy and get to the safety of *The Big Easy*. Then I could work on the problem of finding

Joe and my parents. I wasn't going to come ashore again until I knew exactly where to find my brother.

If we got to the Survivor Radio station, there could be information about where he was. His message had been broadcast on Survivor Reach Out so somebody must know which camp the message came from.

I wanted to learn Joe's location and send a message to Lucy. The rest didn't matter to me. Tanya, Jax and Sam were on a mission to save the country but just a glance at the nasties following us along the road told me the country was already fucked.

If it was true that America was virus-free, then that was my ultimate destination. I wanted to sail there with Lucy, Joe and my parents. My lack of navigational skills meant I couldn't guarantee if we would hit the coast of Florida or end up in Maine but anywhere was better than here. This place now belonged to the army and the virus. Let them fight it out. I wanted no part of it.

It would be a couple of hours before we reached the marina at this speed. I sat back in my seat and closed my eyes. The dream of reaching America with my family and Lucy seemed too far away to even think about.

I couldn't think past the cold reality of our current situation.

I had no idea where Lucy was.

My family was trapped in an unknown Survivors Camp.

We were driving to a marina guarded by the military.

And our only weapon was a herd of fifty zombies.

Fifteen

ALMOST TWO HOURS LATER, WE reached the marina. The road we were on hit a crossroad ahead then carried on down a slope to the waterfront street where the marina shop was located.

We could see the cliffs ahead and beyond them, the rough sea churned beneath dark clouds.

Tanya looked at the zombie horde in the rear-view mirror. They still followed us. They were slow but relentless in their shambling pursuit. "We need to ditch the Land Rover," she said. Her voice was tense.

There was no sign of the army and we couldn't see the beach without going to the edge of the cliff. We knew they were down there, though. We knew we were putting ourselves in danger if we went down there.

We had to lead the zombies down the slope if we were going to create a diversion. Without the diversion, we had no way of stealing a boat.

"Everyone, get ready to bail," Tanya said tightly. She pressed the brake, stopped the Land Rover and got out.

We all did the same. The zombies, seeing us on foot, moaned with hunger.

"What are we going to do?" I asked. "Just walk down there?"

"Do you have a better idea?" Tanya arranged the straps on her backpack and set off towards the crossroads.

The herd was getting closer.

With the zombies behind us and the army in front of us, we were truly between a rock and a hard place. I felt my hands trembling. My mouth was dry and my stomach felt queasy. Why had I agreed to this?

I held my baseball bat loosely, all too aware how useless it would be against guns.

The zombies had reached the Land Rover. They skirted around it, showing no interest in the abandoned vehicle. Their glaring yellow eyes were fixed on us, their intended prey.

"Let's move," Sam said, marching after Tanya.

Jax and I quickened our pace and we caught up with Tanya. There was a tense atmosphere in the air and I knew it was because of the seriousness of our situation. We were walking into an outpost of soldiers who would not hesitate to shoot us.

The order must have gone out to kill any civilians not in the camps. As far as the authorities were concerned, we may be alive now but we were probably going to get turned sooner or later. Better to kill us now and save the army having to fight us later when we joined the rotting ranks of the undead.

We reached the crossroads. The road ahead dipped down to the sea. A small white sign had the words, "Beach Road" on it in raised black letters. In days gone by, that sign had probably brought joy to the faces of children who had come here on holiday. Now, it made me feel sick to my stomach.

We descended the slope to the street below. I had an urge to run to the marina shop and grab all the boat keys there but we had to slow our pace to make sure all the nasties followed us.

The street was deserted but I could see the beach beyond the shops. Soldiers milled about on the sand, guns slung over their shoulders. A collection of Land Rovers and APCs was parked on the asphalt and the sand.

A shout went up and the sound of shots cracked the air.

They had seen the undead herd.

As they ran towards us, I led my companions along the street, past the supermarket and across the road to the marina shop.

I risked a quick glance over my shoulder, expecting to see the zombies shuffling towards the soldiers but the sight at the end of the street made my blood run cold.

The zombies were heading for the shops, shambling in through the open doorways.

They were easy targets for the soldiers.

More shots rang along the street and the zombies started falling as head shots blew their rotted brains out through their decaying skulls.

"Why aren't they attacking the soldiers?" I whispered to Tanya.

"I don't know," she replied, "but this isn't creating a diversion at all. The soldiers are just picking them off. Why are the zombies taking cover?"

Then everything became clear as a cold drop of water hit my arm, followed by another.

Our plan had failed.

It was raining.

Sixteen

I PUSHED OPEN THE DOOR of the shop and we got inside quickly, staying low and in the shadows. The shop was quiet and gloomy. I doubted anyone had been in here since I had hidden from the feral survivors.

Outside, the rain came down with a vengeance, lashing against the windows and battering on the glass door.

We sat in the darkness, leaning against the wall. An air of frustration hung over the group and it was completely understandable. We had spent hours luring zombies here to distract the military only to have them take cover from the rain and cause no problem at all for the soldiers.

"Now what do we do?" I asked.

"We could wait until it gets dark," Jax suggested. "Sneak out there and try to get a boat before they spot us."

"Or just wait until the rain stops," I said. "Those zombies will come pouring out of the shops. The soldiers will have to deal with them."

Tanya shook her head. "We've lost the element of surprise. They'll deal with them easily now. Listen."

Beyond the windows, shots continued. The zombies were being destroyed as they took cover. Soon they would all be dead—our only advantage lost because of the weather.

"So we're trapped here," I said.

"This sucks, man," Sam added.

Tanya was quiet. She looked around the shop. "Does that door lead to the boats?"

I nodded. "Yeah. There's a gravel beach that leads down to the water. The boats are all out there, tied to the jetties."

She crept forward on her hands and knees and retrieved a small pair of black binoculars from the floor. Staying low, she shuffled to the windows that looked out over the marina and cautiously lifted her head. She frowned and brought the binoculars to her eyes, scanning the beach.

She adjusted the focus and whispered, "What the hell?"

"What is it?" Sam asked.

"I…don't know. There are only a couple of soldiers on the jetties. Everyone else is on the beach. There's a big tent there. I don't know…take a look."

Sam crept forward and took the binoculars. "What the fuck are they doing, man?"

The curiosity was killing me. I found a pair of binoculars on the floor and trained them on the sandy beach. The rain smeared the window and made it hard to see clearly but almost all of the soldiers were gathered outside a large olive tent.

They were lined up outside in the rain, filing in when they were called. Two Land Rovers parked next to the tent had the army medical symbol on their doors, a red cross in a white square.

I adjusted the focus and concentrated on a soldier coming out of the tent. He rubbed his arm gingerly through his combat jacket.

"They're being inoculated," I said. "They must have a vaccine or something." Was it possible they had a vaccine against the virus?

"That doesn't matter right now," Tanya said. "They're all over there on the beach. I count four soldiers on the jetties, two on each. This is our chance." She went over to the sales counter and rummaged around until she found a bunch of keys. She brought them over and spread them on the floor.

Five silver-coloured keys, each on a ring that also held a round neon yellow plastic float, so the keys wouldn't sink if dropped overboard, and a white plastic tag stamped with a number. On the reverse of the number tag was the slogan, "Sail To Your Destiny" written in dark green script.

I arranged the tags so they were all number-side up.

42.

45.
59.
63.
71.

"Can we see any of these boats out there?" I asked, pointing my binoculars towards the moored boats.

Tanya did the same. "I see *71*," she said. "It's tied to the jetty on the right, closest boat to the shore."

"That means we'd have to sail it out past all the other boats before we got out to sea," I replied. "Keep looking."

"We need to hurry," Jax said, "Some of the soldiers are coming back."

At the moment, there were only two soldiers on each jetty. They stood in the rain with their weapons slung over their shoulders. They looked bored. I didn't intend to provide them with action to relieve that boredom. If possible, I wanted to sneak past them unnoticed.

I hurriedly scanned the names and numbers on the boats. "I see *42*. She's all the way out at the end of the jetty. Near the fuel pump."

Tanya adjusted her binoculars and searched for the boat.

Jax sounded panicked. "We need to move."

"There're four soldiers coming this way, man," Sam said.

"Let's go," Tanya said, opening the door. "We'll go for 42 but bring all the keys just in case." She scooped them up and went out into the rain.

I followed her out. As soon as I got onto the pebbled beach, I was soaked. The cold rain hissed down onto the beach and the sea. Tanya was headed for the jetty but I caught her arm and pointed to the yellow rowboat lying on the pebbles.

It was the boat I had tried to take out once before. The tide had brought it back in and beached it. We went over to it and glided it into the water before climbing aboard.

Sam took the oars and began to row us out, keeping to the sterns of the moored boats to provide us with more cover.

I hoped the rain and boredom had dulled the senses of the soldiers on the jetties.

We were silent as we slid through the waves. The water slapped against the hull of the rowboat and the oars made splashing sounds as Sam raised them dripping from the sea but none of us spoke or even dared whisper.

I focused on the stern of boat number *42*. Beneath the number, the boat's name was painted in blue. *Lucky Escape*. I gripped the wet wooden edges of the rowboat tighter and willed it to go faster. We were exposed out here. What had made me think trying to sneak a bright yellow boat past soldiers was a good idea? My poor judgement could kill us all.

A moment later, as I was still gripping the edges of the rowboat and trying to concentrate only on the *Lucky Escape*, a shout went up from the jetty.

The soldiers on the jetty nearest us were hidden by the boats tied in their slips but the soldiers on the opposite side of the marina had seen us and were shouting and pointing.

"Fuck!" Tanya said, hitting the side of the rowboat in frustration.

The soldiers across the marina unslung their weapons. I could hear the soldiers closest to us running along the jetty, their boots pounding the wooden slats as they tried to get into a position where they could see us.

"We're going to have to swim for it," Tanya shouted. "If we stay in this boat, we're dead."

As if to confirm what she was saying, a bullet smacked into the hull of the rowboat.

We all jumped.

Seventeen

THE FREEZING WATER SHOCKED MY body as I went under. I surfaced, gasping for breath.

More shouting erupted from somewhere close.

I swam for boat number 42 along with Tanya, Jax and Sam.

There was so much splashing, I wasn't sure if we were still being fired at.

Tanya got to the *Lucky Escape* first. She lifted herself out of the water and climbed the stern ladder with ease. As she vaulted onto the aft deck, she leaned over and shouted at me. "Come on, Alex!" She began fumbling with the keys, searching for the ones labelled *42*.

I couldn't swim any faster. The weight of my clothes dragged me down and swimming while holding a baseball bat was difficult.

"Untie the boat!" I shouted. A mouthful of salty water rushed into my mouth, making me gag. I spat it out and continued swimming.

Tanya darted to the front of the *Lucky Escape* and untied the ropes.

I looked toward the jetty. The two soldiers had almost reached the boat. They would be on the *Lucky Escape* in seconds.

Tanya climbed up the ladder to the bridge as Sam reached the stern. He pulled himself up onto the aft deck and untied the tire iron from his backpack.

The *Lucky Escape*'s engine coughed then died.

I heard Tanya curse from the bridge.

The engine spluttered again.

This time it started.

The water behind the boat churned up as Jax reached the ladder and got on board. I was almost there.

The two soldiers reached the bow and stepped onto the boat, their rifles waving at Sam and Jax. The two military men were young, probably in their early twenties. One had dark close-shaven hair, the other brown. Both looked nervous.

"Hey!" the dark-haired soldier shouted. "Stop!"

They moved forward.

Sam and Jax raised their hands. Sam still held his tire iron in his right hand.

While the dark-haired young man trained his weapon on Sam and Jax, the fair-haired soldier took a radio from his jacket and held it to his mouth. "This is Williams.

We've got two people on a boat here. On the South jetty. Over."

The reply came immediately. "Detain them. Do not let them get away. We'll be there in a minute. Over."

"Copy that," Williams said. "Over and out."

I reached the lowermost rung of the metal ladder that led up to the aft deck. Williams had said two people. The soldiers across the marina knew there were four of us but Williams and his companion hadn't seen us. They didn't know about me or Tanya.

I gripped my bat in one hand and curled my fingers around the metal ladder. Tanya, Sam and Jax had made it look easy to get on board the *Lucky Escape* in a matter of seconds but I knew it would take me a lot longer to pull myself out of the water and climb those few rungs then get over the chrome safety rail at the top. By the time I got up, I'd be shot easily.

Tanya dropped down out of the bridge and I heard scuffling. One of the soldiers shouted then dropped over the side into the water. His rifle, still clutched in his hands, fired a burst of three rounds. I reflexively flattened myself against the boat but the bullets hit the jetty, slamming into the wood with a trio of rapid *thunk*s. The soldier splashed into the sea.

I climbed the ladder.

When I reached the top, Williams stood with his back to me. Tanya was poised in her fighter's stance and Sam brandished his tire iron while Jax held her bat tightly.

Williams had no idea I was behind him.

I swung for his legs, hitting him on the backs of his knees.

He let out a grunt of surprise and went down to the deck, his gun toppling over the side of the boat.

"Get us out of here!" Tanya shouted to me.

I went up to the bridge and got the boat into reverse, backing away from the jetty slowly and turning the wheel to point our bow out to sea. Through the rain-smeared windows, I could see at least a dozen soldiers running up onto the jetty.

I took us out of reverse and increased the throttle as much as I dared to take us out of the marina. When the *Lucky Escape* started to move forward, I increased our speed.

As we left the jetty behind, I let out a breath of relief but we still weren't in the clear.

Shouts from behind us were followed by the sharp *crack* of rifle shots.

"I can't believe they're firing on us when we have one of their soldiers on board, man," Sam said. "That's fucked up."

I looked back. Half a dozen soldiers were firing at us while the other half ran back along the jetty. The dark-haired soldier, Williams' companion, was pulling himself out of the water and climbing one of the jetty ladders.

Either we were out of range or the soldiers were bad shots; none of their bullets hit our boat. When we increased the distance between us and the marina, they stopped trying and stood watching us.

I looked down at the aft deck. Sam was standing over Williams, looking towards the marina. He said to Williams, "Can you swim, man?"

Williams nodded.

Sam pushed him over the side.

Williams went under for a moment, surfaced, then started a slow breaststroke back to shore.

"You shouldn't have done that," I shouted down at Sam.

He looked up. "Why not? He said he can swim."

"We could have got some information out of him. We could have found out what they were doing in that tent."

Sam sighed. "You should have said that, man."

He dived over the side and started swimming towards Williams in a fast front crawl.

What the fuck was he doing? Didn't he realise we had to get out of here? I slammed the *Lucky Escape* into neutral and we bobbed on the waves of our own wake as the rain continued to lash down on deck.

Not that it mattered. We were all soaked to the skin from our dip in the sea. I shivered with cold.

Sam reached Williams and grabbed him around the neck, dragging him back through the water like a lifeguard rescuing a drowning victim. Faced with superior strength and size, Williams seemed resigned to his fate and let Sam bring him back to the boat.

Tanya and Jax helped get Williams on board and sat him on the cream-coloured, padded vinyl bench that ran around the bow.

I went down the ladder.

Sam looked at me. "Well, he's here, man. Ask him your questions and we'll throw him back overboard."

Williams looked up at me with defiance in his eyes.

"Are you going to answer our questions?" I asked him.

He said nothing.

"Look, this isn't a prisoner of war camp," I said. "There isn't a war on and we are not enemies. The zombies are our enemies. We're survivors of a terrible event and we should work together. Don't you agree?"

Williams remained silent. He probably didn't want to get back to shore and have to tell his superiors he had given us information.

I sighed. "Okay, Williams, listen to me. If you don't tell me what was happening in that tent on the beach, we'll throw you overboard but we'll wait until we've sailed out to the middle of fucking nowhere."

Sam looked at me, horrified. Luckily, Williams couldn't see his face.

"You may be able to swim for a while," I said, "but eventually you'll get tired. And then it'll all be over."

Williams looked down at the deck but said nothing.

"Okay," I said, "I'll start the engines."

I started to walk to the bridge ladder.

Williams' voice was low and weak, resigned. "They gave us a vaccination," he said.

I turned to face him. "Tell me more."

He shrugged. Keeping his eyes locked on the deck as he struggled between the need for self-preservation and orders from his superiors, he said, "I don't know what it was. They said it would keep us alive if we got bitten."

"Who gave you the injection?"

"The army medics."

"Where did they get the vaccine?"

He looked up at me. "How should I know? The government, I suppose. Probably some scientists."

I thought about what Jax had said about Apocalypse Island. If her story was true, the vaccine had probably been developed there. Did the fact that the army had a vaccine prove the existence of Apocalypse Island? Not necessarily. It proved there was a government still active somewhere and they were still pulling the strings but Apocalypse Island could still just be a myth.

"Are they vaccinating the people in the Survivors Camps?" I asked Williams.

He shook his head. "They're doing the military first. Then they'll get around to…"

"They'll never inject the ordinary people," Tanya said, stepping forward. "The best way to control them is through fear."

"They will inject the survivors," Williams said, looking at Tanya earnestly.

She shook her head and raised an eyebrow. "Do you believe everything you're told?"

He looked down at the deck again.

"Listen," I said, "do you know what the Survivors Board is?"

He nodded. "Yeah. It's a list of all the survivors in the camps."

I leaned closer to him. "Where is it? Where can I find it?"

"You have to go to a camp. It's on their computers."

"You mean it's a database?"

He nodded. "The survivors in the camps can ask if their relatives and friends are still alive and the soldiers in charge consult the database."

"And it's in every camp?" I asked.

He nodded. "As far as I know."

"How do they keep the list updated, man?" Sam asked.

"I don't know much about it," Williams said, "but I think each camp updates it if someone dies or new arrivals come to their camp."

"You mean it's networked?" Sam asked.

Williams nodded.

Sam rubbed his chin. "Holy fuck, there's a network." He looked at Tanya and Jax.

I rolled my eyes. They probably wanted to take that over as well as Survivor Radio.

"Okay, we're done with you, Williams," I said.

Sam stepped forward to throw him over the side but Williams held his hands up. "No need for that. I'm going." He dived over the side and started swimming for shore.

I turned to the others. "Let's get…"

Something splashed into the water thirty feet off our bow. It exploded and the sea fountained up to join the falling rain. A second later, we heard a deep *boom* from the beach.

"They're firing mortars at us!" I shouted, running for the ladder and climbing up to the bridge. I took us out of neutral and increased the throttle. The waves from the explosion hit us and the *Lucky Escape* rolled from side to side. I held onto the wheel and turned our nose into the waves, increasing the throttle as the boat steadied.

Another explosion off the port side seemed closer, maybe twenty feet away. The accompanying *boom* reached us after the sea had erupted in a fountain of salty spray.

Again we were battered by the sudden high waves. The spray from the explosion hit the bridge windows like watery bullets, streaking over the glass. I slammed the throttle up to max and headed for deeper water, turning south in a gradual arc.

The next explosion hit twenty feet behind us. The spray soaked us but at least the *Lucky Escape* was intact.

I took her deeper. The shore was so far away now that the soldiers were no more than dark dots on a dark yellow band of wet sand.

The mortar fire ceased.

I sat back in the pilot's chair and breathed a sigh of relief when the marina disappeared from view. Keeping close enough to see the shoreline through the rain but far enough away to feel safe from guns and mortars, I kept us on a southerly bearing.

If the military presence at Swansea was anything to go by, the army would be in full force at Falmouth Harbour.

They might even have boats. If that was the case, we were dead. The plan might have to be changed before we got to Falmouth. It might be safer to get to Truro over land.

There was a radio fixed to the wall. I switched it on and Britney Spears' voice filled the bridge, singing about someone being toxic.

I wondered if the vaccinations they were giving the military could really protect them against a zombie bite. If it could, that meant the scientists probably knew what the virus was, how it reacted in the human body.

It probably meant they had prior knowledge of it.

Apocalypse Island.

The evidence pointed to the existence of such a place.

Tanya appeared at the top of the ladder. "Hey," she said, climbing in next to me.

"Hey," I replied.

"We're going to have to get some food from somewhere," she said. "The boat is empty. There's a kitchen but no food."

"It's just a hire boat," I replied. "I guess the customers had to bring their own food on board."

"So show me how this works," she said, pointing to the instrument panel.

"You want me to show you how to pilot her?"

She nodded.

"Okay, but I only know the basics. My friend showed me once, so we could still pilot the boat if anything happened to him."

She gave me a sideways glance and I realised she was asking me to show her for the same reason Mike had shown me. If anything happened to me, they would need to know how to pilot the *Lucky Escape*.

As I talked Tanya through the gauges and controls, Britney finished singing and Johnny Drake's smooth voice came over the airwaves. "That was Britney Spears and 'Toxic'. Now here's a song that goes out to all the survivors still out there. It's Journey and 'Don't Stop Believing'."

As the music began, I wondered if we were really going to be able to get into Johnny Drake's studio and take over Survivor Radio.

Trying not to think of how difficult getting to Truro was going to be, I continued showing Tanya how to pilot the boat.

In case I didn't make it.

Eighteen

WE SAW THE VILLAGE ON the coast two hours later. Tanya was at the wheel, holding our course steady. The rain had eased to a light drizzle then disappeared completely and the dark clouds had blown inland to be replaced by fluffy white cumulus in the deep blue sky. The sun was doing a good job of evaporating the raindrops on the foredeck of the *Lucky Escape* where I sat watching the water and the distant coastline.

My hoodie and jeans were laid out on the deck along with a selection of clothing from everyone else. The fabric steamed in the heat. Sam had stripped down to his boxers and prowled around the deck looking like a modern day Tarzan, if Tarzan sported a soul patch. Tanya and Jax were in their bras and panties. They were both lean, muscled and toned—a pair of action girls who wouldn't look out of place on the cover of a comic book.

I was the odd one out. I was in my boxers but unlike Sam, I had decided to keep my "Sail To Your Destiny" T-shirt on my body. It was uncomfortable and clung to me but I felt less self-conscious than I would if I were shirtless.

Besides, in the sun and breeze, everything was drying pretty quickly.

A gull dived into the waves and came up with a fish, reminding me how hungry I was. My mouth tasted of salt from the mouthful of sea water I had swallowed earlier.

The first indication of the coastal village was a small bay up ahead. The beach there was sandy and rocky with a small gravelled area beyond where two cars were parked. From there, a road led inland, flanked by grey stone houses.

I shouted up to Tanya, "There's a village ahead. Might be worth checking out."

She nodded and cut the engine. The sudden silence made me realise how comforting the constant hum of the engine had been. It was a reminder of civilisation. We had been sailing along, powered by manmade machinery, a link to the old world before the apocalypse. Now we were just floating on a piece of fibreglass and wood, playthings of the elements and the tide like ancient tribespeople paddling a fragile raft into a storm.

The anchor dropped, splashing heavily into the sea. The *Lucky Escape* shifted slightly then settled on the gentle waves.

Tanya came down the ladder and stood on the aft deck shielding her eyes from the sun. "Looks promising," she said, scanning the village. She went into the living area and brought out the binoculars she had taken from the marina store. She inspected the village through the lenses. "I can't see much except the beach, two cars, and a few houses."

"A good place to look for food," Jax suggested.

I nodded. "We need supplies and it doesn't look too bad from here. Maybe it was evacuated or something. Maybe the army cleared the people out and moved on."

Tanya lowered the binoculars. "It looks pretty isolated. Maybe the army never came here and everybody in the village is still there, hiding in their houses."

"Or turned," Sam added. "An isolated village full of zombies. That would make a good horror movie."

As if we weren't already living in a horror movie day by day. I had tried to imagine the village as deserted, all the houses empty, but now Sam's comment worried me. The village seemed almost too quiet. It was dry and warm so there should be at least a few nasties roaming the beach or the road.

I remembered the zombies Lucy and I had encountered on *The Hornet*. Unable to reach humans, they had waited for their victims to come to them, biding their time until the time was right to strike and spread the virus.

Did a rotting, undead corpse lurk behind every door of every house in the village? If so, going there was suicide.

"We don't have a choice," Tanya said as if reading my mind. "We need food and this looks as good a place as any. Alex, you and Jax take the Zodiac and see what you can find."

The Zodiac was a dark blue and white inflatable boat that was tied to the foredeck. It had a small outboard motor and looked like it could carry four people. I didn't know why Tanya had decided Jax and I should take it ashore. Wasn't there strength in numbers?

"We'll empty the rucksacks so you can take those with you," Tanya said. "Bring back as much as you can carry."

"And if we get in trouble?" I asked.

"Then run back with as much as you can carry."

I didn't find her remark funny but I wasn't about to argue. She knew how to pilot the boat now. I wasn't really needed. I certainly didn't bring strength to the group and my ultimate goal was different to theirs. They wanted to get a message out to all the survivors; I only wanted to reach Lucy and find my brother.

If I argued too much or became a burden, I could find myself being thrown overboard like Williams.

So I went over to the Zodiac and started to untie it. It looked sturdy enough. It had an aluminium floor and a bench seat. The sides were inflated but looked sturdy enough. There was a logo that said "Zoom" on the sides and on the front. The engine that had been fitted to this one was small but the craft was light so I guessed it would go fast enough for our purposes, as long as that didn't include outrunning army mortars.

Jax had put her jeans, boots, and white T-shirt on. She came over to help me.

"I hope you don't mind going with me," I said.

"You watch my back and I'll watch yours and we'll be okay," she replied, untying a cord and pulling the Zodiac free.

I put my damp jeans and boots on and the four of us carried the inflatable boat to the rear of the *Lucky Escape*. We got it over the side and when it was in the water, Sam tied it to the aft ladder. Jax and I descended the ladder and climbed on board.

I sat on the bench and Jax knelt by the outboard motor while Sam went to fetch our weapons. He returned with our baseball bats and handed them down to us. I lay them on the aluminium floor of the Zodiac.

Tanya threw the four empty rucksacks down and I stowed them next to our weapons.

"You want to take anything else with you?" Sam asked, offering us his tire iron.

I shook my head. "No, I'm fine with the bat." I didn't want to be weighed down by anything except a backpack full of food. Jax also refused the offer of his weapon and started the outboard engine.

It was noisy and spat out white smoke that smelled of oil and petrol. Jax grabbed the tiller and guided us away from the *Lucky Escape*.

The Zodiac cut through the water towards the beach.

As we reached the sand, I jumped out and waded ashore with the boat's mooring rope. Someone had tied a heavy rock to the rope already so I made a hole in the sand and buried the rock in it. I didn't want to risk the boat floating away with the tide.

Jax tilted the engine forward to keep the propeller from hitting the sand and rocks then she grabbed the empty backpacks and baseball bats and jumped out to join me on the beach.

We slung the backpacks over our shoulders and stood silently on the sand for a moment, listening and evaluating our situation.

All I could hear was the gentle rush of waves breaking on the beach. A slight smell of rotting meat hung in the warm air but that didn't necessarily mean there was a village full of zombies here.

Jax looked at me. "You ready?"

I nodded with more confidence than I felt. "Ready."

We moved up the beach to the parking area. One of the cars was a white Nova, the other a metallic red Toyota Camry.

As we approached, a sudden movement in the Nova surprised us both and we jumped back. Two rotting blue-skinned faces appeared in the back window of the car, their hateful yellow eyes fixed on us. They banged on the windows with their fists, leaving smears of blood and flesh on the glass.

"Don't worry, they can't get out," Jax said. "They scared me though."

"Yeah," I said. The sudden appearance of the two zombies worried me. They had waited there quietly until we were close. If not for the car windows, they would have grabbed us.

How many more of them were hiding in the village?

We readied our bats and walked past the cars towards the houses.

Nineteen

THE VILLAGE WAS NO MORE than a single street lined with thirty or so houses built of grey stone and with small fenced-off front yards, a post office and a pub. The street was deserted. A few cars were parked here and there but there was nothing to indicate that anyone was in the houses. Most of the curtains were closed and through the windows where they weren't, I could only see glimpses of empty living rooms. A dead meat smell hung in the air.

"It's too quiet," Jax whispered.

"Let's just find some food and get out of here," I suggested.

She nodded. "Which house do you want to try first?"

I indicated the nearest house with open curtains. For some reason, the houses that had closed themselves off from the street seemed more dangerous. What if the people in them had closed the curtains as they had fallen ill and died? What if they were roaming the rooms behind those curtains?

"Let's go," Jax said. Then she saw something at the end of the road and put a hand on my arm. "What's that?"

I looked up the road. Past the houses, the street intersected with a wider road that was probably what was considered to be a main road in this rural area. Beyond that road, a low stone wall marked the boundary of a field. Part of the wall was missing. It looked like a vehicle had driven off the road and into the field. Beyond the gap in the stones, a green army truck lay on its side.

"I wish we'd brought the binoculars," I said. "I can't see it clearly. Looks like an army truck."

"We should investigate," Jax said, setting off along the street.

Walking farther from the beach, from the Zodiac, didn't seem like a good idea to me but I had no choice. I couldn't let her check out the army vehicle alone. I caught up with her and kept a wary eye on the houses we passed as we made our way along the street. I was keenly aware of the growing distance between us and the Zodiac.

The pub was called The Fisherman's Rest. Its wooden sign was dark green with the pub's name in gold letters beneath a painting of a fishing trawler sailing on a sunlit sea. I looked into the windows. It was gloomy inside. I could see the bar and the beer pumps and a few tables. There was no movement.

We reached the main road and looked both ways. The road wound between stone walls and hedges in both directions, following the coast. We crossed to the gap in the stone wall and looked into the field beyond.

The army truck bore the medical red cross symbol on its doors. It lay on its side in the long grass and judging by the skid marks on the road and the distance the truck had slid into the field, it had been moving quite fast when it crashed through the wall.

The rear of the truck was crumpled on one side and the windows and windscreen of the cab were smashed. I couldn't see anyone inside either in the front or the rear.

"Do you think it's been there long?" Jax asked.

"A while," I said. "See how the grass behind the truck is standing up? That would have been flattened when the truck slid through here."

"What do you think happened?" She leaned on the wall to get a closer look but neither of us suggested going into the field to investigate closer. Standing here in the dead quiet of a sunny afternoon with the silent village behind us and the crashed army truck lying in the grass seemed almost surreal.

"Maybe somebody in the truck turned, grabbed the driver, sent the vehicle skidding through this wall. Or they might have swerved to avoid hitting something in the road, overcorrected, and gone into the field. We'll probably never know."

"We should check it out," Jax said. Her tone made me wonder if she was trying to convince herself.

"Yeah, we should," I replied. I hated to admit it but there could be something valuable in the truck. Assuming the survivors of the crash hadn't been evacuated by the army when they realised one of their trucks was missing and came to find it, there could be dead soldiers in there. Maybe even guns.

We stepped through the hole in the wall and into the long grass. It swished around our knees as we walked slowly towards the truck. I gripped my bat tightly. My breathing had quickened since stepping into the field and I felt a little queasy. Sometimes these trucks were used to transport soldiers. Any minute now, a dozen of them could come crawling over the tailgate, mottled blue hands reaching for us.

The back of the truck was dark. I knelt in the grass and peered into the blackness. I was sure there were no zombies in there waiting for us and the air here didn't smell any worse than it did on the road.

Jax had gone around to the cab. "There's nobody up here," she said, "but there's something you should see."

"Okay, be there in a minute," I replied. I didn't want to go up front without first checking that the rear of the truck was empty. The tailgate was held shut by a metal pin on each side that had been dropped into a hole in the truck's metal frame. I turned my bat over in my hand and used the handle to push first one pin out then the other. I hooked the lip of the bat's handle over the tailgate and pulled.

The crumpled metal refused to move at first. I pulled harder and it opened with a metallic scream.

I stepped back so quickly, I nearly fell over in the grass.

My heart slowed slightly when I saw no zombies. There was a mess of papers, medical equipment and cardboard boxes in there but no bodies, either dead or undead.

I went around to the cab and joined Jax. She pointed at the shattered windscreen. Some of the shards of glass were blood-stained. There had probably been more blood but the rain had washed most of it away.

"I expected to see blood," I said. "Somebody was driving the truck when it crashed."

"So where are they now? There aren't any bodies."

"Maybe the army sent out a search party when this truck didn't arrive wherever it was headed. They evacuated the casualties." I thought about that for a moment then changed my mind. "No, I don't think that's what happened. There are medical supplies and papers in the back. They wouldn't leave them behind."

"What if the driver turned and crawled out?" Jax asked, scanning the long grass. "Or what if he's still alive? He could be somewhere in this field. He could be watching us."

We both stepped back instinctively.

I watched the grass for movement but if there was anyone out there, he was taking care to keep still. A line of trees marked the edge of the field a quarter of a mile away. Could an injured man crawl out of the truck and make it that far? I shielded my eyes from the sun with my hand and stared at the trees but I didn't see anything resembling a man or a corpse…or a walking corpse.

"Let's get some of the stuff out of the back of the truck then get out of here," I suggested.

Jax agreed and we went around to the back. With the truck lying on its side, everything had fallen out of the metal racks that were fixed to the walls and ended up in a chaotic heap. Jax kept watch while I went into the truck on my hands and knees.

I grabbed handfuls of loose papers and tossed them out to Jax. "Take a look at these, they might be useful." It was too dark inside the truck for me to read anything. I grabbed one of the cardboard boxes and threw that out the back too. I found a hardbound notebook and two first aid kits in green plastic boxes. I dragged them back outside and examined the notebook in daylight.

The cover was dark green with a white label that had the words, "Sgt. Wilder" written in it in black pen. I flicked through it. Inside there were dates and notes written in black ink. I stuffed it into one of the backpacks along with the first aid kits.

"These papers are useless," Jax said, "They're just lists of names and dates." I looked at a few of the sheets. The names were printed onto the paper and next to each one was a handwritten date. Vaccination dates?

"What's in the box?" I asked.

She reached into the box and pulled out a clear plastic packet that contained a small sealed glass bottle of amber coloured liquid. I took it from her and inspected the bottle. It was clear and unlabelled. The top of the bottle was sealed with a metal lid which had a rubber seal in the centre for inserting a hypodermic needle.

"The vaccine," I said.

Jax nodded. "I'll put it in my backpack."

I went back into the truck and searched through the jumble of items until I found a box of needles still in their packages with hard plastic covers over the sharp tips. I grabbed a handful and brought them outside. I stuffed them into my backpack along with the first aid kits and notebook.

Jax had stopped looking at the papers and was staring at the trees on the edge of the field.

"What's wrong?" I asked, getting up and adjusting the backpack straps.

She pointed at the trees. "There's a man over there."

I looked over at the area. Before I had gone into the truck, there had been nobody among the trees. Now, a man stood watching us. He was too far away to make out any details but something about him unnerved me.

"We need to go," I said to Jax as I backed towards the hole in the wall.

"Definitely," she whispered. "Why is he just standing there watching us?"

"I don't know."

We reached the road and again I was all too aware of the distance back to the safety of the Zodiac.

The man stepped forward out of the trees and into the sunlight. He didn't move like a zombie. He was alive. I could make out his combat jacket and trousers. Was he the driver of the truck? Maybe he had staggered off to the trees after the crash. He might have suffered a concussion.

He began walking then picked up the pace and ran through the grass towards us. His arms and legs pumped in strong quick motions as he moved faster, seemingly fixed on us.

"Run!" Jax said, turning on her heels and sprinting for the village.

In a blind panic, my heart beating so hard I could feel it in my temples, I chased after her.

Behind me, I could hear the *swish, swish, swish* of the grass as the soldier ran through it to reach us. Then I heard his boots on the road, the soles pounding the tarmac relentlessly as he pursued us.

I wasn't going to make it to the beach. Jax might have a chance; she ran with strong fluid strides and her petite frame flew along the street. But I wouldn't reach the Zodiac before the soldier caught me.

Jax suddenly veered left, leapt a picket fence and veered between two houses. I followed, almost snagging my jeans and falling when I jumped the fence. I got a quick glimpse of the soldier behind me. He was fifty feet away, still moving like an Olympic sprinter. I fled down the side of the house around to the back door.

It was open. Jax had smashed the lock and was in the kitchen trying to drag a big wooden table over to block the door. I ran inside, closed the door, and helped her bring the table over. We got it behind the door and both of us dropped to the floor so we couldn't be seen through the kitchen window.

The soldier's boots pounded around the house and into the back yard, slowed, then stopped. Jax and I looked at each other. I saw my own fear reflected in her eyes. I dared not move a muscle in case the soldier in the yard would hear and come crashing through the door.

He was no ordinary man. I had no idea what he was but I knew he was not normal. I closed my eyes and tried to recall the glimpse I had of his face when I had stumbled on the fence. There had been something wrong with his skin, something strange about his eyes.

But he was not a zombie; zombies did not move like that. The virus controlled the host's basic motor functions and the result was a slow shamble. The soldier outside had covered a quarter of a mile in less than two minutes.

I couldn't hear any more sounds from the back yard. Was he out there listening for us? Waiting for us to make a move?

If I wasn't breathing so hard from the run, I would have held my breath. The only sound in the kitchen was the low hum of the refrigerator.

We sat there for what seemed like five minutes before Jax whispered, "I think he's gone."

I nodded. We slowly got to our knees and peered out of the window. The back yard was empty. The overgrown grass had been stamped down in places but the soldier was gone. There was nothing out there but a child's pink swing set. I wondered if the child who owned it would ever use it again.

Twenty

WE EXPLORED THE HOUSE QUICKLY and made sure it was safe. It looked like a typical family had lived here once. The family photos showed a couple in their thirties and a bright eyed blonde girl of eight or nine.

The upstairs consisted of a simply-furnished double bedroom, the little girl's bedroom decorated in pink, and a spare room that was being used to store cardboard boxes full of books and DVDs. The bathroom was tidy and decorated in sea blue with plastic fish and crabs on the window sill.

Downstairs we found a utility room and a cozy living room.

A typical family house.

I wondered where they were now.

We found food in the kitchen cupboards and filled the backpacks with cans and jars. We wouldn't be going hungry for a while.

As long as we could get this stuff back to the *Lucky Escape*.

We left the food-stuffed backpacks in the kitchen, went into the living room and sat on the sofa after shrugging off our backpacks full of medical supplies. The curtains in here were closed and I left them that way. If the soldier was out there roaming the street, there was no point risking him seeing us through the window.

"What the hell was he?" Jax asked. "He wasn't an ordinary soldier. There was something about him…something strange."

"I got a glimpse of him," I replied. "His skin and his eyes were weird. I don't know exactly what it was, I only got a quick look."

"You mean he's turned?"

I shrugged. "He can't have. We know how the zombies move and it isn't anything like that. It was like being chased by Usain Bolt."

"You think he's still out there?" she asked, looking at the curtains.

I nodded. "Somewhere."

"He must have been the driver of the truck."

I dug into my backpack and found the notebook. "If he is, he's probably Sergeant Wilder. This is his notebook." I laid it on the glass coffee table and opened it.

Flicking through the pages, we discovered that Wilder had been tasked with transporting the vaccine from a nearby army base to the medics who were vaccinating soldiers at the outlying military outposts. Reading the list of places he logged in the book, we learned that the army had men stationed at every major port, harbour and marina.

He hadn't worked alone. Wilder was part of a team called Alpha 3 Victor. Along with Wilder, the other team members were Corporal Francis and Lance Corporal Jones.

Judging by the dates entered in the notebook, the vaccination program had been in operation for just over two weeks.

The final entry was dated two days ago and Wilder had written a simple note in the margin. "Cpl Francis was bitten four days ago. He has not turned but keeps saying he wants to be left alone. Tries to wander off at every opportunity. He doesn't look well but at least he hasn't become one of the nasties."

There was nothing else in the book that could help us piece together why the truck was lying in a field and one of the team had chased us into the village. Where were the other two members? There were no bodies in the truck so either all three men survived the crash or they weren't all in the vehicle when it went off the road.

I closed the notebook. "How are we going to get back to the beach with him still out there?"

STORM

Jax thought a moment then said, "Let's take a look out of the upstairs windows. We might be able to come up with a plan if we know exactly where he is."

We went upstairs. The double room and the spare room looked out over the street. We tried the double room first, parting the curtains and looking down onto the street.

He was there, pacing up and down along the row of houses like a tiger ready to pounce.

"Look at his face," Jax whispered.

It was difficult to see his features clearly at this angle but I could see the veins in his neck and face were abnormally dark blue. His skin did not have the blue mottled colour of the zombies, which made the veins stand out even more in contrast. The backs of his hands were the same, dark blue veins spreading like an inked spider web from his wrist to his fingers. His eyes were the same yellow as the eyes of the other zombies.

He didn't move like an undead zombie being controlled by the virus. He moved like a living man and that made him all the more dangerous. We knew how fast he could run. There was no way we could get to the beach, untie the Zodiac, and be on the water before he caught us.

"What are we going to do?" I asked Jax.

"I have an idea," she said, leaving the room and going into the pink-wallpapered girl's room. The window looked out over the back yards of the houses. Jax pressed her face against the glass and looked in the direction of the beach. "We'll have to go the back way," she said.

I looked out at the row of yards. Each small patch of grass was separated from the next by a waist-high wooden picket fence. I remembered how I had stumbled on the front yard fence. This time I would be weighed down with a backpack full of heavy cans. It didn't seem like a good plan to me.

"I don't think I'll make it," I said.

"We're not going to run. We're going to sneak down to the beach."

The thought of going outside while the soldier was out there sent a chill down my spine. "Can't we just wait awhile? He might go away."

She looked at me with sympathy in her eyes. Sympathy seemed to be the default emotion I brought out in girls. "I'm scared too, Alex, but we have to get back to the boat."

"I just don't think I'm going to make it if I have to outrun him with a backpack full of food weighing me down."

She didn't say what we were probably both thinking—that a backpack of food wasn't going to make the slightest difference. I would be too slow to escape this hybrid soldier zombie even if I had on a pair of Nikes and running gear and no backpack at all. I just wasn't built for this shit. The neglect my body had suffered from so many years of sitting on my ass while playing video games and eating crap wasn't just going to go away overnight.

The reason didn't really matter. All that mattered now was that if I went out there, I would probably get killed.

Or bitten. Or eaten. Or whatever that hybrid intended to do to his victims. Either way, I wasn't happy about leaving the house while he was out there on the street.

"You go," I said to Jax. "I don't think there's any point in me even trying."

"I'm not going to leave you here," she said.

I didn't know how to respond to that. I turned my head away when I felt hot tears in my eyes and wiped them away with the back of my hand.

"How about we get something to eat while we're making our plans?" Jax asked.

I nodded and we went downstairs to the kitchen where we found burgers in the freezer. We got a pan of water boiling on the stove top and added rice to it while the burgers cooked in the oven. I got one of the cans of baked beans we couldn't fit into our backpacks and poured the contents into a saucepan.

The smell of cooking burgers made my mouth water. They sizzled and spat in the oven and I could hardly wait to get them out and start eating.

While I took charge of the rice, beans and burgers, Jax explored the house more closely than our initial inspection.

"What are you looking for?" I asked as she rummaged through the cupboard beneath the sink.

"A gun would be nice."

"Good luck finding one of those."

She continued searching, pulling out cleaning cloths, bottles of bleach, and a plunger.

"You going to plunge him to death?" I asked.

She smiled and said sarcastically, "Very funny."

"I don't think we're going to find anything that kills hybrid soldier zombies," I said.

"You think that's what he is?" she asked, getting to her feet and leaning against the wall by the stove. "A hybrid?"

I shrugged. "I have no idea. All I know is he looks like he has the virus but unlike the other zombies, he's still alive. The virus is controlling him and using him to spread itself to other humans but it hasn't killed him. Probably because he was vaccinated before he got bitten."

She frowned. "Was he bitten, though? I can't see a wound on him."

She was right about that. Most of the zombies had very obvious wounds where they had been bitten when they were alive. Blood-stains on their clothing told the story of how they had ended up as part of the undead horde. But the soldier seemed to be bite-free. So how had he contracted the virus?

"I don't know," I admitted. "Without taking a closer look, we probably won't ever know. And I'm not volunteering to go out there and inspect him for wounds."

She nodded and left the kitchen to see what she could find in other parts of the house. I heard her open the door beneath the stairs and start a search in the storage area there.

Twenty minutes later, the food was ready. I found plates and put them on the counter before filling them with rice, beans and burgers. Jax appeared at the doorway. "Smells good."

"Yeah. We can't eat it at the table since the table is blocking the back door so I suggest the coffee table in the living room."

"Sounds good."

We took our food into the living room and sat on the floor at opposite ends of the low table while we ate. The food brought my taste buds alive and I savoured every fork full.

"You find anything?" I asked Jax between mouthfuls.

"Not much. A pair of old binoculars, a hockey stick, tennis rackets, and some fishing equipment under the stairs. Some kid's toys. Nothing else that could even be remotely useful."

The mention of fishing equipment reminded me of the days on *The Big Easy* fishing with Lucy. Those days seemed so long ago now and I was almost sure I would never see Lucy or *The Big Easy* again. Getting a message to her on Survivor Radio seemed like an impossible task. We couldn't even get out of this house, never mind travel to the radio station and take control of the airwaves.

"The fishing stuff will be useful," I said. "We should take that with us."

She nodded. I knew what she was thinking: *Take it with us how exactly? You're too unfit to leave the house.*

We ate the rest of the meal in silence. I wondered how Jax had been affected by the apocalypse, how many loved ones she was missing. It seemed to me that Jax, Tanya, and Sam might have given themselves this mission to take over Survivor Radio to distract them from the reality of the situation. They must have family unaccounted for, people they loved who could be alive, dead, or somewhere in between. Yet all three of them seemed to be full of bravado and a tough inner strength.

Maybe they were just tougher than me. They were the type of people who were into extreme sports and martial arts. Competitors. Survivors. These were mentally and physically equipped to survive a zombie apocalypse.

A sudden idea hit me.

"You ever play tennis?" I asked Jax.

She nodded. "I used to when I was younger."

"Were you any good?"

"Yeah, not bad. Why?"

I ran the plan through my mind again. It could work.

I said, "I think I know how we can get out of here."

Twenty-one

I STOOD IN THE DOUBLE bedroom with the binoculars pressed against my face. I wanted to get a better look at the hybrid soldier. He had stopped prowling around and now he stood as still as a statue in the middle of the street. When he came into focus, I saw the bite on his neck. He had been bitten by a zombie after all but the wound was slight. Most people were almost torn apart by the zombies that killed them and the resulting wounds were deep and bloody.

The soldier had a simple set of bloody marks on his neck shaped like a set of teeth. I wondered how he had been turned. According to the notebook, Corporal Francis had been bitten already but Wilder's note said Francis did not turn. He just wanted to be left alone and tried to wander off. Maybe Wilder and Jones were taking Francis back to base and Francis did finally turn and attacked them. The truck went off the road and Francis bit the other members of the team. But if that was the case, where were they? Why hadn't all three members of Alpha 3 Victor been in the field near the truck?

I lowered the binoculars and went to find Jax. She was in the little girl's pink bedroom, sitting on the bed and staring out of the window at the gathering gloom of the approaching evening. She had a faraway look in her eyes and again I wondered who she had lost in this apocalypse, who she was missing.

"Hey," she said when she saw me.

I told her about the bite on the soldier's neck then added, "So he was bitten but the vaccine kept him alive, turning him into a hybrid. He's infected with the virus but it hasn't killed and reanimated him. Also, I think it takes them longer to turn when they've been vaccinated. It sounds like it took Corporal Francis four days. I think he bit Wilder and Jones, causing the crash."

She caught on to what I was thinking. "The last note in the book was written two days ago. So you think that's Francis out there on the street and Wilder and Jones are still turning somewhere?"

I nodded. "Probably somewhere in that field. Or in those trees where Francis was standing."

She thought for a moment then said, "This is bad, Alex."

"Yeah, all the soldiers are being vaccinated. How many of those soldiers will get bitten by zombies? How many have already been bitten since they were injected with the vaccine?"

"There's going to be thousands of zombie hybrids just like Francis," she said. "The shambling dead ones are bad enough but now we're going to have to deal with runners as well."

"The virus will spread, a lot faster," I said.

She nodded then said, "Let's get out of here."

We went downstairs to the kitchen. On the table we had placed the tennis racket from under the stairs and four tennis balls. I had no idea if this was going to work but it was our best chance to get back to the Zodiac. Evening was already falling. Tanya and Sam probably thought we were dead. I just hoped they hadn't sailed away and left us in this godforsaken village.

I helped Jax put on her backpack and she helped me do the same. We would have to carry the second backpacks we each had and we were prepared to dump those if we had to. We were hoping we wouldn't have to.

Carefully, we lifted the dining table and moved it away from the back door. Jax took the tennis racket and balls out into the back yard while I went into the living room and parted the curtains just enough to see the soldier.

He stood watching the street. Did he even remember what he was looking for anymore or was he waiting for any stimulus to spark him into action?

I turned to see Jax in the back yard holding a tennis ball in one hand, the racket in the other. She tossed the ball up with a graceful movement then brought the racket up swiftly. The ball went sailing over the roof of the house.

I turned back to the hybrid soldier. He was as still as he had been a few seconds ago. Then I saw the vibrant green tennis ball land in the yard of a house across the road and bounce against the living room window with a bang.

The soldier turned to where the sound had come from. He moved a step forwards, then another and another until he was walking to the yard across the street.

A second ball sailed into the street and landed on the roof of a Volvo before bouncing away down the road.

Walking quickly, the soldier reached the Volvo and looked into the windows of the car.

Jax sent the third and fourth balls in rapid succession down the street, trying to lure the soldier farther away. With no other sound or movement to stimulate his senses, he followed the balls although he didn't seem as interested now, as if he might have realised they were not worth pursuing.

I went through the house and out into the yard. "Let's go," I whispered to Jax.

We went to the first fence and placed the backpacks we were holding over into the next yard. We had packed towels between the cans so they wouldn't make much noise but the sound of everything settling in the packs as we put them on the ground sounded too loud. I was sure the soldier would hear us. If he heard us now, we were dead.

STORM

Carefully, we straddled the waist-high fence and climbed over. It was difficult with the weighty pack on my back shifting every time I moved but I got over into the next yard and picked up my second pack. Jax was already waiting at the next fence. I looked at the row of yards ahead of us. There were at least a dozen fences between us and the last yard in the row. I groaned inwardly.

It took us nearly an hour to move along the yards. It was slow and strenuous work, lifting the packs over each fence and listening for the approach of the hybrid soldier. I had no reason to believe the soldier had some sort of super-hearing but even so, every little noise we made sent my heart hammering. I was bathed in sweat by the time we climbed out of the final yard. The sky was darkening into twilight with a few stars already visible.

We stood a hundred feet from the parking area where the white Nova and the red Toyota Camry sat. The Nova was as quiet as it had been when we first arrived, the zombies inside hiding and waiting for unsuspecting prey.

We pressed ourselves against the side of the house. We had no idea where the soldier was. He could be at the far end of the street or he could be standing just around the corner. Our ruse with the tennis balls had gotten us this far but now we had to run for the Zodiac. As soon as we stepped away from the side of the house, we would be visible and vulnerable.

I slowly leaned out and peeked around the corner of the house, half expecting to see the soldier standing right in front of me, yellow eyes glaring. But he was still at the other end of the village, standing still in the road. And he was facing in the opposite direction, toward the field and the crashed truck, his back to us.

I whispered to Jax, "He's looking the other way. If we're quiet, we can get to the boat."

She nodded and we broke cover, walking toward the beach and carrying our heavy packs as quietly and as quickly as possible. I kept looking over my shoulder, afraid that the soldier would turn and see us, but he remained still as a statue staring the other way.

The tide had gone out and the Zodiac, which we had left in knee-deep water, now rested on the damp beach. The mooring rope lay twisted on the wet sand like a dead snake.

"Shit," Jax whispered.

"We can drag it to the water without making too much noise," I whispered back. "If we…"

A sudden noise to my right startled me. The zombies in the Nova had erupted into action and were banging and clawing at the car's windows.

The soldier standing on the street turned slowly, saw us, and started running towards the beach.

We fled to the Zodiac, dropping our second packs and weighed down by the ones on our backs.

I grabbed the wet coil of rope and yanked it with all the strength I could muster. The rock anchor came out of the wet sand with a sucking sound. I threw it into the boat. It clattered on the aluminium floor.

STORM

We picked up the boat and side-stepped to the water as fast as we could. I glanced along the street. The soldier was less than a hundred feet away.

Splashing into the sea, we pushed the boat into deeper water and climbed on board. Jax fumbled with the engine, pulling at the starting cord with trembling hands.

The hybrid zombie soldier had reached the cars. The zombies in the Nova detected movement and went crazy but he ran past them, his deadly focus on us.

Jax pulled the starter cord again.

The engine burst into life, coughing out clouds of oily smoke.

The smell of gasoline had never been so sweet.

The soldier splashed into the sea, still running at us.

Jax grabbed the tiller and the engine roared. The Zodiac leapt forward so quickly, I almost went overboard, saving myself from such a fate by gripping the seat until my hands hurt.

We sped out into deeper water.

The hybrid soldier stopped when he was up to his waist in the sea. He stared at us with a malevolence that made me shudder.

Jax slowed our speed and steered us for the *Lucky Escape*.

I breathed deep breaths of salty air tinged with the smell of gasoline. We were safe.

I watched the soldier as he turned and strode back up the beach. He reached the white Nova and banged on the rear side window with his fists. The zombies inside were going crazy, clawing at the window.

The soldier smashed his fists through the glass and grabbed the closest zombie. He tried to drag it out through the small opening but the arm and head ripped away. He tossed them onto the ground and reached in for the second zombie, pulling it out viciously.

The rotting zombie tore apart as it was forced through the small window opening.

The soldier crouched down over the zombie parts on the ground, selected an arm, raised it to his mouth, and ate.

I leaned over the side of the Zodiac and puked violently into the sea.

Twenty-Two

THE FOUR OF US SAT in the living area of the *Lucky Escape* around the small table. The radio was on and Survivor Radio was playing a selection of rock hits. Beyond the windows, darkness had fallen and the lights inside the boat cast a pale light over the room.

We had eaten a dinner of pasta and tomato sauce and Jax and I had told Tanya and Sam about our experience in the village. They had listened intently, asking questions now and then and getting us to clarify parts of the story so they knew every detail. The appearance of the running zombie hybrid was big news. This changed things. If we were going to have to deal with hordes of runners as well as shamblers, the danger factor in our mission went up several thousand notches.

When we finished telling our story, Sam shook his head as if in disbelief. "That's some fucked up shit, man."

I couldn't have put it better myself.

A sudden noise on the windows startled us but it was only rain hitting the glass.

"That's another thing," I said, "the hybrids won't take shelter from the rain like the other zombies have to. The hybrids are alive. They aren't rotting away so the virus doesn't need to protect them in the same way. That soldier chased us into the sea without a second thought."

Tanya sighed. "So they're some sort of super zombie and the rain won't protect us anymore."

I nodded. "That's what it looks like."

"Any idea how many of them there could be?"

"It's impossible to know for sure. But if everyone in the military is being vaccinated, that's a lot of people walking around with the potential to become a hybrid. Since they work dangerous jobs and come into contact with zombies all the time, a lot of soldiers must get bitten or scratched every day."

"So we're screwed," Sam said. "There's going to be an army of undead hybrids."

"Except the hybrids aren't undead," I said, "They're alive."

"Does it make a difference, man? Either way, if they catch you, you're fucked."

"Yeah, that's true." I leaned back in my seat and closed my eyes, feeling a wave of despair flood over me. There was no way we would survive on land once the number of hybrid runners increased. What was going to happen to the people in the Survivors Camps? I thought about Joe and my parents. How could they possibly survive a hybrid attack on their camp? And where was Lucy? For all I knew, she had been captured by the soldiers and was also in a camp somewhere.

I needed to get that message to her on Survivor Radio but it seemed an impossible distance away now that there were nasties, soldiers and hybrids between us and the radio station.

"How does this affect our mission?" Jax asked nobody in particular.

"It doesn't," Tanya replied immediately. "We need to get the message out to the survivors even more urgently now. They're in even more danger than they were before." She looked at me and asked, "Based on what you know of this vaccine, do you think we should we inject ourselves with it?"

The three of them looked at me expectantly and I realized that I did have a role in this group after all. They were strong and fit and intelligent but they saw me as being smarter than them. While they had spent time in exotic places filming adventurers like Vigo Johnson, my life had consisted of playing video games and reading books, many of which pertained to exactly the situation we now found ourselves in.

Games and books were one thing and real life was another but my knowledge of a zombie apocalypse...even based on fictional works...was better than nothing. It allowed me to make guesses about our situation that were informed opinions…even though the information came from the thoughts and ideas of writers and game designers. I wondered how many of those writers and game designers were now dead and how many had lasted long enough to see their nightmares come to life.

I thought a moment about Tanya's question. "There might be an advantage in vaccinating ourselves," I said. "If we get bitten without the vaccine in our blood, we'll die quite quickly and the virus will reanimate us as zombies. If we get bitten after we've been vaccinated, it takes around four days to turn. If nothing else, that will give the rest of us time to decide what to do with the infected person."

"That's easy," Tanya said. "We kill them."

"It might not be that easy. When vaccinated people get bitten, they try to isolate themselves. Wilder's notes said Corporal Francis kept trying to wander away, saying he wanted to be left alone. The virus probably makes the host do that so the host isn't vulnerable during the incubation period. So it isn't easy to kill them. They might just disappear, go into hiding somewhere, then reappear four days later as a hybrid." I closed my eyes and rubbed my forehead, trying to reconstruct Corporal Francis's transformation into a hybrid in my mind's eye.

"I think that when a nasty bites a vaccinated person," I said, "it stops after the initial bite. It doesn't tear them apart like it would normally. The soldier we saw had a single bite on his neck. Maybe the nasty gets a taste of the vaccinated blood and stops. That means the host has a good chance of surviving. He goes somewhere remote and becomes a hybrid, infected with a mutated form of the virus. Either the original virus reacts with the vaccine or it mutates itself to turn the victim into a zombie despite the vaccine, the same way certain strains of bacteria become resistant to antibiotics."

"Dude, you're geeking out on us now," Sam said. "I think we should vaccinate ourselves. At least that gives us four days after being bitten. And we get to stay alive. That beats death and reanimation in my book."

Tanya looked at him with hard eyes. "You're assuming we'd let you live for four days after you got infected."

He shrugged. "Like Alex says, I'd get the hell out of Dodge and the next time you saw me I'd be a kick-ass hybrid."

She rolled her eyes. "You sound like you want to be a zombie."

"Nah," he said, "the hours suck. But I'd rather be a living hybrid than one of those mindless dead fuckers."

Tanya considered that and nodded. "I think we should all be vaccinated."

"It's safer," I agreed. "If nothing else, it means we won't get ripped apart by zombies. They'll deliver one bite then leave us alone when they taste the vaccinated blood."

Jax spoke up. "If that's the reason the soldier only had one bite. For all we know, he could have killed the zombie that bit him before it could sink its teeth into him again. It might not have anything to do with the vaccine."

I nodded. "That's true. We don't know."

"If you get bitten, you're screwed either way," Tanya said. "The best course of action is not to let them bite you."

"I'll drink to that," Sam said, raising his mug of water. He took a gulp then looked around the table. "I had medical training before I did the survival shows with Vigo. So I can give the injections. Who's first?"

Ten minutes later, we had all been injected with the amber liquid. It hurt like a wasp sting as it went in and the area on my shoulder where the needle had gone in rose into an angry red welt.

Sam vaccinated himself last, then disposed of the used needles and empty vaccine vials in the kitchen trash can. "Man, that stings," he said. "I wonder what's in that shit."

Jax, rubbing her shoulder, said, "You'd have to ask the scientists on Apocalypse Island. They made that stuff just like they made the original virus."

Unwilling to listen to another political rant, I went out onto the sun deck and looked up at the stars. The rain had stopped for a moment and the night breeze was cool. I could hear an animated discussion inside as my three friends talked about their favourite subjects: the government, Apocalypse Island, and conspiracy theories.

What did it matter where the virus came from? It was too late for that knowledge to do us any good. When you were burning in the flames of hell, knowing who lit the match wasn't going to ease your pain.

When the rain started again, this time as an insidious drizzle, I climbed up to the bridge and sat in the pilot's chair. Thousands of raindrops streamed down the windows like tears, blurring my view of the coast and the sea.

It was only later, when I went back down the ladder to the deck after letting my thoughts about the apocalypse, hybrid zombies, Joe, and Lucy run in depressing circles, that I saw a soldier on the beach. He was alone, half-running, half-stumbling over the wet sand. He looked drunk as he weaved across the beach to the base of the rocky cliffs.

I went back up the ladder to get the binoculars from the bridge and brought them back down to the deck. Adjusting the focus, I watched the soldier as he dropped to his knees then curled up into a fetal position, shivering as if he had hypothermia.

He wasn't shivering from the cold. He wore the usual army outfit, including a waterproof camouflage jacket, and the night was cool and wet but not cold enough to make anyone shiver. He was obviously infected. He had left his squad somewhere up on those cliffs and come down to the deserted beach to turn.

As he lay there shivering, I understood why vaccinated victims of the virus sought out a remote place to turn. They were weak and vulnerable while the virus and the vaccine fought a biochemical war inside their bodies. There was a risk that they could be easily killed so the virus compelled the host to find a safe place to turn.

If the host was sick like this for four days, maybe there was a good chance they would be killed before they turned. If the military knew about the four days downtime, they might be hunting down and killing the hosts before they had a chance to complete the transformation into hybrids.

Even if they weren't being killed by the army, it was possible that not every infected host completed the transformation. Maybe in some cases, the vaccine won the biochemical battle and the host did not turn.

Maybe they lived through the four days and beat the infection.

Or maybe the strain on the body killed them.

I lowered the binoculars. I didn't want to look at the shivering, curled up soldier any longer.

I was vaccinated now and if I got bitten, that was the fate that awaited me. Lying helpless and alone while the virus tried to take over my body.

I went back inside. Even listening to the three amigos talk about Apocalypse Island was preferable to seeing that lone figure on the deserted beach.

And wondering if I was going to end up like him.

Twenty-Three

BY NOON THE FOLLOWING DAY, we had sailed around the southern tip of England and begun to make our way north along the English Channel. Grey clouds scudded across the sky, occasionally breaking and showering us with cold rain. The day was grim and the sea was rough. The *Lucky Escape* rode the waves well but every now and then a swell would break over her hull and the decks would be drenched with a deluge of saltwater.

I sat in the pilot's chair, making sure we stayed deep enough to avoid rocks but also close enough to shore that we didn't go off course. Jax stood looking out of the water sheen that covered the bridge windows. Tanya and Sam were somewhere in the living area, keeping dry. I had the radio on but even Johnny Drake must be in a depressed mood today; he played mostly emo and Goth tracks.

A quiet, contemplative atmosphere had descended over the boat. We were all lost in our own thoughts of the mission ahead. I was wondering if it was even possible to get to the radio station alive. The slogan painted on the boat's hull and printed on my T-shirt, "Sail To Your Destiny" seemed particularly apt today. And the destiny wasn't good.

Jax had come up to the bridge five minutes ago, said, "Hi," and then stood silently watching the coastline through the windows. I wasn't sure if she wanted a conversation or not so I kept my mouth shut. If she spoke to me, I would answer. Otherwise, I was going to stay quiet.

The silence didn't bother me too much. I was used to uncomfortable silences with girls.

After another minute of staring out at the rain and cliffs, she said softly, "Do you think we're going to make it, Alex?"

I sighed. Did she want a truthful answer or reassurance that everything was going to be OK? I decided to walk the middle ground and said, "I don't know." If I had tried to reassure her, I wouldn't have sounded convincing at all and if I had been truthful, I would have said, "No, Jax, I don't think we're going to make it. I think we're all going to end up dead…or worse. We don't have a chance of surviving this crazy mission."

She turned to face me. There were tears in her eyes. "I don't want to die." She wiped her face with the back of her hand.

"Me either," I replied. "So let's try and stay alive." I sounded much calmer than I felt.

She smiled and nodded. "Good idea."

I was about to reply but she held up her hand, silencing me. "Do you hear that?" she whispered.

I listened. All I could hear was Bauhaus singing "Bella Lugosi's Dead" on Survivor Radio. "The music?" I asked like an idiot.

"No, not the music," she said, twisting the volume knob to zero.

Then I heard it. Outside. Beyond the windows. Voices. "What's that?" I asked, vocalizing my confused thoughts. It sounded like hundreds of people speaking at once out there. I leaned forward and used my sleeve to wipe away condensation from the window. There were shapes on the cliffs and the beaches.

We went down to the deck where Tanya and Sam were already leaning on the railing and gazing towards the shore.

On the tops of the cliffs and on the rocky beaches, at least a hundred soldiers lay curled up beneath the slate grey sky. They all lay in the same fetal position and they all murmured the same three words. But they weren't saying the words in unison so the sound they made as a group was confused. I listened to the jumbled torrent of words and picked out what each soldier was saying. "Leave…me…alone."

Tanya turned to me. "What's happening?"

"They've all been bitten," I said. "And because they're vaccinated, the virus is battling with the vaccine. They'll be like that for four days then become hybrids…or die." I shrugged. "I don't know for sure."

Sam stared at the curled up soldiers with fascination in his eyes. "Why do they keep saying that? 'Leave me alone'? It's fucked up, man."

"They're probably just saying that because it's the only thought going through their heads. The virus compels them to find an isolated place and they're vocalizing the command." The voices floating across the water to our boat were eerie. The soldiers sounded distressed, in pain.

I remembered the soldier I had seen on the beach last night. He had been silent.

"I think they're only murmuring like that because they're in close proximity to one another. Look at that one down there alone on the rocks." I pointed to a soldier who had removed himself from the others and lay alone on the beach. He shivered like the others but his mouth was closed and he made no noise.

It seemed the words, "Leave…me…alone," were an automatic reaction to the presence of others.

I went back up to the bridge and turned on the radio again. Those eerie voices were creeping me out. On the radio, Johnny Drake had switched to a more upbeat selection of tracks and was currently playing "Summer of '69" by Bryan Adams.

I watched the soldiers through the water-streaked windows until we sailed past them and their voices faded away in the distance.

An hour later, the sea calmed and the *Lucky Escape* settled into a gentle rolling gait as she took us along the Cornish coast towards Falmouth. I checked the map and guessed we would be approaching the harbour in the next thirty minutes. I cut the engine and went down to the deck where the others were sitting.

"We're approaching the harbour," I said. "What's the plan?"

Tanya looked at the late afternoon sky. "We should wait until it's dark before we sail past the harbour into the river. It's our best chance."

Everyone agreed so I went back up to the bridge and took the *Lucky Escape* out into deeper water and continued toward Falmouth. We could get a look at the harbour from a safe distance and wait there until dark. The plan didn't fill me with confidence but I couldn't come up with anything better and I knew that if I didn't go through with this, my chances of seeing Lucy again were probably zero.

When a wide inlet appeared, cutting a path inland, I used the binoculars to see more details. A small castle sat on the headland. I wondered if the army were using it as a lookout post but it looked abandoned. The harbour was situated on the other side of the headland, which meant I would have to sail into the wide inlet to assess the situation there. I just hoped we weren't sailing into a trap we couldn't escape.

I piloted the *Lucky Escape* around the headland and into the inlet. Despite the huge size of the inlet, having land on both sides of the boat made me feel claustrophobic.

The harbour appeared on the port side. It was much larger than the marina at Swansea and the area was filled with boats of all shapes and sizes moored to the long jetties. I couldn't see any soldiers. The harbour was eerily quiet. The rain became a weak drizzle then stopped entirely.

The mouth of the river that led inland to Truro lay directly ahead. Maybe I should make a run for it now while there seemed to be nobody around. I had feared a huge military presence but the lack of even a single soldier unnerved me. I thought I could see army vehicles parked in the harbour but it was hard to tell from this distance.

On the water, something sparkled in the afternoon sun like a silver spider's web stretching across the mouth of the river all the way to the nearest jetty in the harbour.

Using the binoculars, I took a closer look.

What I saw made me groan. An emptiness filled my gut as I realized I was going to have to tell the others the bad news.

As soon as I climbed down the ladder and stood on the deck in front of them, they knew something was wrong by the expression on my face.

"What is it, man?" Sam asked.

"We can't take the boat past the harbour," I said.

They were silent, waiting for me to continue.

I said, "The army have barricaded the river."

Twenty-four

WE TOOK TURNS LOOKING THROUGH the binoculars and we all came to the same conclusion. Our plan was dead in the water.

The army engineers had built a barricade that stretched all the way from the harbour jetty and spanned the river. It floated in the water, a ten-foot-high steel wall supported by huge plastic barrel-shaped floats. It looked like it had been put together in sections and the movement of the water made it undulate like a living, breathing steel snake.

At the harbour, army Land Rovers and personnel carriers were parked in clusters but none of us saw any soldiers. The area seemed quiet but from this distance we probably wouldn't be able to hear any sounds that far away. All we could hear was the slapping of waves against the *Lucky Escape*'s hull.

We went into the living area and sat around the table to decide our next move.

"What do we do?" Tanya asked.

"We could go over land," Sam suggested.

"Too risky," Jax said. "We have to get past the barrier and take the boat upriver. There's no other way."

"We can't get past it," he replied. "And there might be even more barriers farther up the river. We'd be stuck, man. Easy targets for the army to blow out of the water."

"I don't see any soldiers," Tanya said. "Maybe they've all gone away to turn into hybrids or something."

"That is possible," I said. "If the harbour was attacked by hybrids, the soldiers could all have wandered away to find a place to turn." I thought about that a little more. "If that's the case, we can get past the barrier by going around it on the jetty and getting into the river on the other side."

"Dude, we have to get the *Lucky Escape* past the barrier too," Sam said.

I shook my head. "No, we don't. We can take the Zodiac. Carry it across the jetty and get into the water on the other side of that wall. If there are other barricades upriver, we can get onto the bank and carry the Zodiac around them too,"

"Portage," Sam said, nodding. "I like it."

"It will make us less of a target than if we were in the *Lucky Escape*," Tanya said. "Let's do it."

"There's just one thing," I reminded her. "The harbour has to be empty of soldiers. Otherwise we'll get captured as soon as we set foot on it."

"Something else," Jax added. "If hybrids attacked the harbour, where are they now?"

We all knew the answer to that; they were probably still there. Waiting.

"We'll check it out closely before we leave the Zodiac," Tanya said. "Everyone grab your weapons."

We went out onto the sun deck and began to untie the Zodiac while Jax used the binoculars to study the harbour. "Plenty of vehicles," she said as we carried the boat to the aft deck, "but I can't see any soldiers."

That was both good news and bad. Good because it meant we weren't going to get blown out of the water by the army. Bad because there must be a reason the soldiers weren't there anymore and that reason could still be lurking at the harbour.

We got the boat into the water and climbed aboard with our weapons. Jax started the engine and the familiar gasoline smell filled the night air. As we set off towards the jetty, I looked back at the *Lucky Escape*. She bobbed on the waves looking abandoned in the fading sunlight. I hoped she would still be there when we got back.

I hoped we would get back.

Tanya had the binoculars and she watched the harbour as we approached. "Looks clear," she said. "I can't see much because of all the boats but the place looks deserted."

Jax guided the Zodiac between two yachts, heading for a set of stone steps that led from the water up to the top of the high jetty. Sam jumped onto the steps and held the boat steady while we clambered out. Between the four of us, we managed to hoist the Zodiac up the steps. The boat wasn't too heavy for the four of us to handle but it dripped cold water over us as we carried it to the top of the jetty.

At the top, we set it down on the concrete and looked around. The barrier had been fixed to the end of the jetty by thick steel braces that looked like they had been embedded into the stone by some sort of huge drill. There was no way we could detach the barricade. It stretched out across the water to the bank on the other side. It was miles long and must have taken days to construct.

I assumed the army had built it to keep boats in rather than keep them out. The river ran all the way to Truro and along the way there were yacht clubs, small marinas and harbours. This barricade would make sure none of those boats sailed out into the channel. It looked like the military really was trying to control everybody.

As I stood admiring the technical work that had gone into erecting such a huge barricade, a sudden silence descended over the harbour. Even the birds stopped singing, just as they had at Mason's Farm.

"No way should it be this quiet," I whispered.

"What's that?" Jax asked, pointing to the buildings on the shore.

I squinted at the place she had indicated. "I don't see anything."

"There," she said. "Oh my God, we need to get out of here! Now!"

Dozens of hybrid soldiers erupted from the cluster of buildings like ants scuttling out of a nest. They ran towards the jetty, fixing us with their hateful yellow eyes. As the first half dozen reached the jetty, more and more came pouring out from between the buildings. I was reminded of a scene in a Matrix movie where thousands of copies of Agent Smith attack Neo.

The soldiers, although different facially, wore identical uniforms and their running bodies blurred into a mass of camouflage patterned jackets.

"Let's move!" Tanya shouted, grabbing the Zodiac.

We all lifted the boat and headed for the steps that led down the opposite side of the jetty but it was obvious we weren't going to make it. "Take it to the end and throw it over," Tanya shouted, changing direction. We took the Zodiac to the end of the concrete jetty and heaved it into the water twenty feet below. The boat landed with a splash and took on some water but remained afloat.

The nearest soldiers were almost on us. Their boots thundered along the jetty.

We all jumped. In normal circumstances, I would have thought twice before diving twenty feet into the sea but with a horde of hybrids running towards me, I didn't even give the jump a second thought.

I hit the water and went under, enveloped by cold and darkness. Struggling to the surface, I heard splashes as other bodies landed in the water around me. I had expected to hear three but there were many more.

I broke the surface and gasped for air. Splashing through the water to the Zodiac, I saw Tanya, Jax and Sam. They were almost on the boat, swimming strongly.

Splashes continued around me, some spraying me with water. I swam like a madman. I was so panicked I couldn't breathe. The hybrids were in the water with me. As I swam for the Zodiac, I heard more of them hit the surface and go under.

My three companions were clambering onto our inflatable boat.

I thought about dropping my bat. It was slowing me down.

Jax, on the boat and pulling at the engine's starter cord, turned to me, her eyes wide. "Alex, swim!"

Tanya and Sam leaned over the side of the boat and reached out their hands towards me.

But as I reached up to take them, a hand grabbed my boot and pulled me under.

Twenty-five

I BARELY HAD ANY BREATH in my lungs as I was dragged down through the murky water. I kicked out with my free foot and my boot connected with something but the hand still gripped me.

I held my bat in both hands and jabbed it down as hard as I could, hoping to hit the hybrid's head and make him let go of me. Instead of letting go, he reached up with his free hand and grabbed my other boot. I was helpless, unable to kick or swim, being pulled down to a watery death. At least I would drown before he bit me. My lungs already screamed for air and my chest felt like it was collapsing.

In a minute, it would all be over. I would never know what happened to Lucy, never find Joe.

A movement to my left startled me. A face and arms appeared, swimming rapidly at me with wide, strong strokes. I wouldn't have thought the hybrids could swim but here was one coming this way to prove me wrong.

It reached me and I turned to look into its yellow eyes.

They weren't yellow.

They were blue.

It was Sam. He turned over and faced downwards before sweeping his arms and diving down towards my boots, tire iron gripped in his hand.

He had come to save me. Sam had risked his own life to save mine.

I wanted to tell him it was too late; the tiny breath of air I had in my lungs was gone.

I couldn't tell him anything. We were underwater.

And everything was turning black.

A low ringing began in my head.

The blackness seeped over my eyes.

Then everything ended.

* * *

The first sound I heard was the cry of seagulls. And voices. Familiar voices. Jax and Sam, talking. I couldn't hear what they were saying but their voices were rushed, panicky. I wasn't concerned. I listened to the Zodiac engine firing steadily. The sound of the boat gliding through the water.

I could smell fish. And the gasoline smell of the engine.

My clothes were wet and cold. I was lying on a hard surface.

Something heavy pressed against my chest over and over.

Now the panic I heard in Sam's voice got into my head. I had almost drowned. The heavy pressure on my chest continued.

I felt a rush of water travel up my throat and into my nose and mouth. I gagged on it, spat it out.

I opened my eyes and saw the night sky and stars above.

My throat felt raw. My nose burned.

Sam was above me, a worried look in his eyes. "He's coming round," he said to someone I couldn't see.

I sat up and leaned against the inflatable side of the Zodiac, gasping for breath.

"How you doing, man?" Sam asked. He sat back on his heels, grinning. Jax was behind me with her hand on the tiller and Tanya was at the front of the boat scanning the water ahead with the binoculars.

"I'm not dead," I said.

Sam laughed. "No way, man. I saved your ass."

"Thanks." I looked over the side of the boat towards the shore. A pair of gulls sat on the water, fighting over a fish that they had torn apart. The shore was no longer the rocky seashore I was used to seeing. It was a wooded bank. The trees came all the way to the water's edge.

I turned and looked at the opposite bank. More trees, with fields beyond.

We were on the river.

"How long have I been out?" I asked.

"Only about a minute, man. Don't sweat it. I hauled you into the boat and started working on you. Jax got us out of there. That was some fucked up shit."

I looked back beyond Jax to the harbour. The yellow-eyed soldiers stood on the jetty motionless, their prey out of reach. I had no idea why some of them had followed us into the water.

"We just learned one thing," Sam said.

"What's that?" I asked.

"That hybrids can't swim worth a damn."

"It doesn't make sense that they'd jump in like that," I said. "The virus doesn't have anything to gain if they die. Why did they do that?"

"Don't ask me, man, I just work here."

I racked my brain for the answer to my own question. I wanted to understand the virus. It was our enemy and if we understood it, we could predict what the zombies would do in specific situations.

So far we had seen that it protected the true zombies—the dead, rotting ones—by keeping them out of the rain. Why would it allow hybrids to jump into the sea like that? Their flesh wasn't rotting so they had nothing to fear from the water itself but they couldn't swim. Jumping into the deep sea was suicide. The hosts were destroyed and could not spread the virus.

It made no sense.

Sam tapped my shoulder, bringing me out of my thoughts.

"Don't dwell on it too much, man. We're alive and that's all that matters."

"Holy shit," Tanya said from the front of the boat. "There're zombies everywhere."

We didn't need the binoculars to see what she was talking about. The movement in the trees on the shore and dark shapes shambling through the fields told us everything we needed to know: this area was crawling with zombies. I couldn't see any hybrids out there, just a whole load of shamblers. A few seconds after we saw them, their low moans came drifting across the water to our boat.

They couldn't get to us but the sight of so many zombies made my skin crawl. The air was thick with the stench of their rotting flesh. Their unnatural gait and staring yellow eyes spoke to some deep fear within me. I could barely stand to look at them as they dragged their putrefying corpses across the fields and between the trees.

Some of the walking dead came down to the edge of the river bank and stood glaring at us. Some stretched out their blue mottled hands and clawed at the air. None of them stepped into the water.

As I watched them, I understood the fundamental difference between these dead shamblers and the living hybrids. The shamblers were totally under the control of the virus. It had killed the host and now controlled the body. In the case of the hybrids, the host was still alive and still had some control.

Even though the hybrids had a primal urge to spread the virus, they also had a remnant of their human emotions. The hybrids at the harbour had jumped into the sea because their desire to catch us overrode the virus's need to keep the host alive.

Their virus-infected brains didn't think, "If I jump into the sea, I will drown". They didn't base their actions on logic, only on the need to kill their prey. They no longer possessed the intelligence to avoid throwing themselves into dangerous situations.

The shamblers had the same lack of intelligence but the virus had complete control of their bodies so it kept them from harm because if the body was harmed, the virus could not be spread by that host.

If the rage of the hybrids meant they acted without self-preservation and ignored the needs of the virus, maybe there was a way to use that against them.

Sam waved his tire iron at the zombies on the riverbank. "You want some of this? Come and get it."

"There's no point taunting them," Jax said.

"I'm ready to bust some heads, man." Despite his outburst, Sam seemed too relaxed for a man on a dangerous mission.

I, on the other hand, was terrified. The countryside was crawling with zombies and we were heading to a city where the undead population would be even larger.

We weren't going to make it out alive.

Twenty-six

WE CONTINUED ALONG THE RIVER into the night. An inky blackness crept across the sky and low-lying dark clouds blotted out the moon. I could barely see the zombies on the bank but their low moans told me they were still there. Apart from the moans, the only other sound was the purr of the engine and the rush of the water against the Zodiac's sides as we glided upriver.

The gasoline smell coming from the engine masked the stench of rotting flesh hanging in the night air.

Tanya, Jax, and Sam were quiet. I guessed they were all wondering what lay ahead and how they were going to complete their mission. In their minds, they had probably already taken over the radio station, got their message out, and were back in the *Lucky Escape* sipping champagne.

I had no such illusions. My three companions might be winners in life but I was used to failure mixed with a good dose of disappointment. I was pretty sure I would never see the *Lucky Escape* again. Or Lucy. My heart broke at the thought of not seeing Lucy again. What had started out as a massive crush based only on her looks had developed into something much more. I didn't think I could bear surviving the apocalypse without her.

Tanya turned to us and whispered, "We've reached the city."

The trees and fields gave way to houses with lawns that stretched down to the river. Beyond the houses, the glow of street lights illuminated hundreds of zombies wandering aimlessly like lost souls.

As we traveled farther upriver, the houses gave way to industrial units and factories then shops and businesses as the river wound into the heart of Truro. The banks of the river became walls of cement and stone with a safety rail that separated the river from a small walking path. The path was heaving with nasties. They glared at us as we passed them.

They were everywhere, clogging up the city with rotting flesh and hungry moans. In the distance we heard a gunshot and I wondered if the army was actually fighting this massive horde of the undead or if there were survivors in the city. Maybe someone had simply had enough and taken their own life. Goodbye, cruel apocalypse.

"We're not going to be able to get off the boat," I said.

Sam said, "We don't need to, man."

I threw him a confused look but the pale overhead lights on the path barely reached our boat so I wasn't sure Sam saw my face in the darkness. I added, "What do you mean?"

"The building we're heading for was BBC Radio Cornwall before the army took it over for Survivor Radio. I came here with Vigo Johnson last year to do an interview about a TV show we had filmed in the Sahara. While we were waiting to go on air, one of the producers was shooting the shit with us and he took us out to the back of the building to get some fresh air. There's a covered walkway out there with a waist-high wall. The other side of that wall drops straight down into the river. All we have to do is climb out of the boat and over the wall. It's simple, man."

It sounded simple but he was forgetting the fact that the building was probably heavily guarded by the military or could be overrun with zombies or hybrids. This was not going to be simple. Rather than give me hope, Sam's optimism pissed me off.

I sat brooding in the boat until we got to the radio station. I felt a mixture of fear, depression, and anger, which made for a bad combination. I didn't even know who I was angry at, only that I felt like smashing heads with my baseball bat to relieve the pressure building up inside me.

"We're here," Tanya whispered.

The river forked into two. On the left, it ran to a small marina with a large store and a zombie-filled parking lot.

On the right, a group of white-painted buildings skirted the water. Both forks ran beneath a wide bridge, along which ran a main road judging by the amount of abandoned cars up there.

The final building on this side of the bridge had black letters on its wall that read, "BBC Radio Cornwall". A porch roof supported by brown-painted wooden struts ran almost the entire length of the building, covering a narrow walkway, which was hidden from us by a low white wall that dropped down to the water.

There was no sign of life. Or zombies.

"It's too quiet," I whispered.

"Would you prefer soldiers? Or zombies, maybe?" Sam asked. He laughed. "Jesus, Alex, you're too highly-strung, man. Relax."

"It doesn't make sense," I protested. "If the army is running their radio broadcast from here, why aren't they guarding it?"

Jax leaned forward and said, "Why would they guard it from the river side? Zombies don't swim."

And nobody else would be crazy enough to do what we were doing.

Jax steered us in towards the wall and Tanya stood up with the Zodiac's mooring rope in her hand. She reached up, grabbed the top of the wall and pulled herself up and over in a swift, graceful movement, crowbar in one hand. She checked the area and tied the boat to one of the porch struts. "It's clear," she whispered down to us.

Sam went next, heaving his bulky frame over the wall. "Pass the weapons up," he whispered to us.

Jax passed our bats and his tire iron up to him then looked at me. "You want to go next?"

"You go ahead. I'll follow." My refusal was nothing to do with chivalry; I wasn't sure I could make it over the wall. It wasn't all that high but for someone as unfit as I was, it was high enough to give me serious doubts that I could pull my bulk over the top. I almost suggested that I stay with the Zodiac but if I did that, I would never be able to get my message to Lucy.

Jax jumped up and pulled herself over quickly.

I stood up in the Zodiac, leaning against the rough, white stone to steady myself. I slid my hands up to the edge of the wall and curled my fingers over the top. I wouldn't be able to do this. I was too heavy.

Tanya, Jax, and Sam grabbed my forearms and pulled me up. I used the toes of my boots against the wall to assist them but it wasn't necessary; they had me over the top in seconds.

I stood in the narrow cement walkway between the wall and the building. Both ends of the walkway were closed off with tall, locked, iron gates. Another reason the army didn't have to worry too much about people climbing in this way.

"Thanks," I whispered to my companions.

"Don't mention it, man," Sam replied. They had pulled me up because they knew I couldn't climb over by myself. I felt both grateful and embarrassed. I picked up my bat and hoped I could prove myself in the fighting ahead. I was tired of being the weakest member in every group.

Sam went to the nearest window and looked inside. "We're going in this way," he whispered. "The studio is upstairs so we need to get up there as quickly as possible." He jabbed his tire iron at the corner of the window. The glass shattered.

I had thought we were going to use stealth but Sam's approach was fast and hard. He reached in and opened the window before disappearing through it into the dark room beyond.

"Go, Alex," Tanya said, pushing me forward. She was making sure I didn't lag behind by making me go in front of her. Luckily the window was large. I struggled through and found myself inside a carpeted room with vinyl chairs and a sofa. Framed Radio Cornwall posters hung on the walls.

Sam opened the door and light spilled in from a lighted corridor. The girls pushed past me and ran out of the room with Sam. I followed, scared to be left alone. I didn't want to be killed or captured and someone must have heard that window breaking.

The corridor was brightly lit with strip lights, the floor covered in blue and grey vinyl floor tiles. Pictures of the Radio Cornwall DJs lined the walls.

At the far end of the corridor I could see an empty reception area and a steel and glass door that led to the parking lot. Two soldiers stood outside the door, looking out into the night. Their rifles were slung over their shoulders and they looked relaxed. If they had heard the window breaking, they didn't seem too bothered by it.

"Alex, this way," Sam whispered, holding a door open for me across the corridor and gesturing for me to follow him. I went through quickly and we ascended a wide set of stairs to the next floor.

A double door at the top was open and two soldiers stood guarding it, facing away from us. Tanya and Sam rushed up the steps and swung their weapons before the soldiers knew what was happening. They crumpled to the hallway floor.

As I reached the top of the stairs, Sam tossed me an assault rifle. I caught it reflexively, being careful to point the barrel at the floor. I recognised the gun as an L85 rifle but my knowledge of weapons came from video games, not from real life. "I've never fired a gun before," I said.

Jax, holding the other L85 and looking like she could grace the cover of *Soldier of Fortune* magazine, said, "It's easy. Just point it and pull the trigger."

"Come on," Tanya said, stepping over the bodies in the doorway.

We followed her along the corridor. I kept the gun pointed down and my finger well away from the trigger. The weapon felt heavy in my hand and I had to carry my baseball bat tucked under one arm. The bat hit my leg as I ran. Jax carried her bat in one hand and the rifle in the other. I considered doing the same but I was worried I wouldn't be able to aim one-handed.

We reached a windowless door at the end of the corridor and Sam opened it. We stepped through into a production studio. The room was dimly lit but an electric glow came from banks of audio machines and computer screens. A plump woman with long blonde hair and wearing glasses, headphones, jeans and a Robert Plant T-shirt looked up from the computer as we entered.

"What the hell?" she asked as she pulled her headphones down to her neck.

"We're not going to hurt you," Tanya said quickly, raising her hands in a placating motion. "We just want to get into the broadcast studio."

A large window above the banks of machines showed the next room where a slim black man in his thirties with dreadlocks and wearing a Jim Morrison T-shirt sat at a desk and spoke into a large microphone. He was surrounded by papers, computers and machines with dials and sliders. He wore headphones and seemed oblivious to our presence as he spoke into the microphone.

"We're broadcasting," the woman said, pointing to a red light above a door that was marked "On Air".

"What's your name?" Tanya asked her.

"Cheryl. Cheryl Ginsburg."

"Cheryl, we're going to put out a message on the radio. Jax here is going to stay with you while the boys and I go in there and meet…Johnny Drake, I presume?"

Cheryl nodded.

"We're not going to hurt anyone," Tanya said. "But we have to make sure our message goes out to the people. So you can just relax and don't touch anything."

Cheryl raised her hands and wheeled her chair away from the computer. Jax levelled her gun in Cheryl's general direction but the woman didn't seem to be a threat at all.

Sam opened the door to the next room and we stepped through beneath the "On Air" light.

Johnny Drake looked up as we entered and his eyes went wide. He ripped off his headphones. "What the hell?" He reached for a dial on his desk but I pointed my gun at him.

Tanya stepped up to the desk. "No, Johnny," she said. "Don't touch that dial."

Twenty-seven

JOHNNY RAISED HIS HANDS IN surrender. "Okay, guys, no need to do anything we'll all regret." It was strange to hear the familiar rich tones of his mid-Atlantic accent in real life when I had heard them on the radio for so long. All the time I had been listening to his show, I hadn't thought about meeting Johnny Drake in person and I certainly hadn't envisioned holding him at gunpoint.

Tanya went around to the desk and looked at the controls and dials. "Get me on air," she said to Johnny.

He nodded. "Okay. Here, let me get this…" Leaning forward, he reached for the control panel.

Tanya grabbed his wrist and looked into his eyes. "Just remember, if you try anything, we've got your friend Cheryl at gunpoint in there." She nodded towards the window. Johnny looked into the production studio where Cheryl sat, arms raised, as Jax stood over her with the L85.

"There's no problem here," Johnny said. "I'll patch you right in and you'll be on every radio that's turned on."

"Do it," Tanya said.

He reached for a switch then hesitated. "You have to realise," he said, finger poised over the switch, "that the army listen to Survivor Radio all the time. It plays in all the Survivors Camps. As soon as they hear your voice, they'll know exactly where you are. There's a whole platoon stationed outside this building. They have tanks and huge guns and the road is totally blocked with razor wire. You won't be able to escape."

"Let me worry about that," she said, flicking the switch.

Johnny leaned back in his chair with a resigned look that said, "It's your funeral," on his face.

"This is a message to all the survivors," Tanya said into the microphone. "Everything you have been told is a lie. The virus has not infected the world, only Britain. The authorities have told you there is no escape so they can control you and put you in camps. They are covering up their own mistake…a mistake that has killed millions of people and means those in charge are mass murderers.

"You have to refuse to be confined by liars. There are options other than sitting in a Survivors Camp waiting to die. The army are attempting to control ports and marinas but they have a problem on their hands right now. There is a hybrid version of the virus that is affecting vaccinated soldiers. Yes, that's right, the soldiers have been vaccinated. Have you? No, they are not going to vaccinate you. Only themselves.

"The hybrids are weakening the military. We saw it ourselves at Falmouth Harbour. All the soldiers there had become hybrids. I won't lie to you, the chances of survival are slim but you can take boats and sail to Europe. Tell them what is happening here. Once the rest of the world knows our plight, they will send help.

"This country has been plummeted into hell by the people in charge and they have told you there is nothing you can do about it because the rest of the world is in the same hell. That isn't true. You can escape. But first you need to escape the camps. Head for the coast. Tell the world what has happened here."

She flicked the switch and stood back from the control panel.

Johnny Drake looked at her. "Is that true?"

"You should know, you're part of their system."

He shook his head. "No, that isn't true. Cheryl and I are prisoners here. We've been kept in this building since the outbreak. We don't know what's happening outside, only what they tell us and what we see through the windows."

We heard tires screeching outside in the parking lot.

"They're here," Sam said. "We need to leave."

"Wait," I said, leaning forward to the microphone and flicking the switch. "Lucy, it's Alex. I don't know where you are or what happened at the marina. Meet me at…" I tried to think of a place I could mention on the radio without alerting the army to where I was going. "…At the place Mike and Elena died. In three days' time." I added, "Joe, if you can hear this, I'm going to find you somehow."

I turned to Johnny. "Did that message go out?"

He nodded.

"We're leaving," Tanya said.

"Take us with you," Johnny said, looking suddenly desperate. "Please."

She hesitated for half a second before saying, "We're going to have to fight our way out of here."

"That's fine. I can't stay locked up in this building any longer."

"Let's go," Tanya shouted.

We left the studio and ran back down the hallway with Johnny Drake and Cheryl Ginsburg in tow. The two soldiers Tanya and Sam had dealt with still lay in the same positions. I didn't know if they were unconscious or dead.

As we descended the stairs, we heard boots running along the hallway below.

We reached the bottom of the stairs and Jax stuck her head and arm out through the doorway, firing her rifle. The bursts of fire cracked the air in the enclosed space and made my ears ring.

Jax sprinted across the hallway into the room we had broken into earlier. She looked across at me. "Alex, put down some suppressing fire!"

I handed my bat to Johnny Drake and shoved my rifle out through the doorway, pointing it along the hallway and squeezing the trigger. It spat out bullets and kicked in my hand. The soldiers in the reception area took cover.

Sam went across the hallway with Johnny and Cheryl as I continued to let off bursts of deadly bullets. The windows in the reception area shattered.

Tanya went across and beckoned me to follow.

I leapt into the room. Sam closed the door and pulled the vinyl sofa across it. "We're out of here, man," he said as he ran for the broken window.

We went out onto the cement walkway one at a time. By the time it was my turn to climb through, the soldiers on the other side of the door slammed into it. The sofa slid across the carpet.

"Give me that," Sam said, grabbing my rifle. He let off a burst of rounds at the door. The pushing from the other side stopped.

Dropping down into the Zodiac was easier than climbing out of it. With six people, it was a tight squeeze but we found our places and sat tight while Jax started the engine and turned us around in a wide arc so we faced downriver.

As we started out of the city in a cloud of gasoline-tinged engine smoke, Sam pumped his fist into the air. "We fucking did it, man!"

I couldn't share his enthusiasm. I was glad to be alive but I had no idea if Lucy had heard my message. The meeting place I had suggested worried me.

The lighthouse where Mike and Elena had met their deaths.

Somewhere I had vowed to never return.

The rain began to fall from the night sky as we approached Falmouth Harbour. I wished the heavens had broken earlier so we didn't have to endure seeing the rotting mass of zombies lining the river banks. I was sick of them. I wanted to take the rifles and fire every last bullet into the crowd of yellow-eyed monsters. It would be a waste of ammunition and even if every bullet delivered a killing headshot, it wouldn't make any difference to the huge population of zombies but it might make me feel better.

Instead of actually carrying out my plan to waste all of our bullets to fight the depression that was dropping over me like a heavy, dark blanket, I just closed my eyes and thought about it while Tanya and Sam filled Johnny and Cheryl in on the events of the last few days.

I had already heard Johnny say that he never had access to the Survivor board—the list of survivors and camps—and that he was given the Survivor Reach Out recordings on data sticks. He had no idea which camp they came from or when they were recorded.

After hearing that, I tuned out.

I needed to get my hands on one of the networked military laptops if I was to have any chance of finding Joe.

The harbour looked as deserted as it had earlier except for the drowned hybrid bodies floating face down in the water by the boats. The ones that hadn't jumped in after us had disappeared. Probably hiding in the shadows of the buildings. The hybrids seemed to go into a dormant state when there was no prey around. They found a place out of sight and stayed there until triggered into action by sound or movement.

I thought back to the hybrid in the village, standing in the middle of the road waiting for us. He hadn't been hiding because he knew the prey was already aware of his presence. But when he first saw us, he was hidden in the trees at the edge of the field.

As we got closer to the metal barricade, I stared at the shadows between the buildings, waiting for a tell-tale movement. There was none.

"We're going to have to get the boat over the jetty," Tanya said. "And we're going to have to do it fast. Those bastards are around here somewhere."

Sam picked up one of the L85s. "No problem, man. We've got guns now."

Tanya picked up the other rifle and nodded. "Only shoot if you have to. We need to preserve ammo."

"You got it," Sam replied.

Jax steered us around the floating bodies to the steps that ran up to the top of the jetty. Sam took the rope and jumped out onto the lowest step, pulling the Zodiac towards him. We grabbed our weapons, Johnny taking Tanya's crowbar and Cheryl picking up Sam's tire iron. We all got out and picked up the boat, carrying it on our shoulders as we ascended the steps. Once we were past this obstacle, we would be back on the *Lucky Escape*. I could hardly wait. My nerves were frayed. I felt exposed out here.

Not long now. Just get across this jetty and we'd be safe.

But as we got to the top of the stairs, all hell broke loose.

Sam was in the lead and he was the first to react. He shouted, "No!" and let go of the Zodiac as he brought his rifle up. The boat crashed down on one side as Sam started firing.

The hybrids were everywhere, getting up from where they had been lying on the cement jetty. They had been silent and patient while we blindly stumbled into their trap.

I realised with a sudden cold clarity that in our absence, they had not gone into a dormant stage at all.

They were waiting for us.

Twenty-eight

THE ZODIAC CRASHED TO THE steps then slid into the water.

Sam brought up his rifle as a hybrid leapt at him. The gun spat twice and the hybrid crumpled at Sam's feet.

Tanya joined Sam and began shooting into the mass of yellow-eyed ex-soldiers. The ones they hit dropped to the cement but there were so many others, it was only a matter of seconds before they would overwhelm us by sheer numbers.

We had no choice but to get back onto the Zodiac. Sam and Tanya were already backing down the steps as they fired into the advancing hybrids.

The Zodiac's rope floated on the water like a dead snake. I grabbed it and pulled the boat closer to the steps.

I didn't need to tell anyone that the Zodiac was our only chance of survival. Cheryl and Jax jumped on board, followed by Johnny and myself. Tanya and Sam came backwards down the steps, the L85s kicking and spitting in their hands. Hybrid bodies littered the steps.

Jax pulled on the starter cord. The engine spluttered and died. She shouted, "Come on!"

Tanya and Sam continued shooting until they both ran out of ammo.

There were still dozens of hybrids on the jetty.

They leapt into the Zodiac and Jax pulled the starter cord again. The engine coughed out a cloud of gasoline smoke. Jax tried again but the engine still did not start.

Sam and Johnny grabbed the metal oars from the floor of the boat and used them to push us away from the jetty before beginning to row us out into the harbour.

We weren't going to put the distance between us and the hybrids in time.

Two hybrids jumped from the steps and grabbed the side of our boat. They attempted to scramble on board but I swung my bat into the skull of the one closest to me and it collapsed into the water.

Sam jammed his rifle butt into the face of the other, sending it sprawling backwards. It still held onto the boat with one hand until Sam smashed its fingers with the butt and the hybrid sank into the depths. Sam picked up the oar again and rowed furiously to get us farther from danger.

Four more hybrids jumped down on us. One of them missed the Zodiac entirely and splashed into the water.

Two landed short but managed to hook their arms over the side of the boat. Sam and I went to work on them. I smashed the bat down on the head of the one closest to me. The impact was so hard it sent a blast of pain through my hands and wrists and up my arm. The hybrid sank into the water, leaving a stain of blood spreading across the surface.

Sam attacked the other with the rifle butt, sending it reeling away.

Behind me, I heard a scream. I turned in time to see the fourth hybrid land in the boat and scramble for Cheryl. She kicked at it but everything happened so fast, nobody else had time to react. The hybrid lunged forward and sunk its teeth into Cheryl's neck. Her scream became a garbled choke as the hybrid's forward motion took them both over the side of the boat into the harbour.

"No! Cheryl!" Johnny cried, reaching for her. She and the hybrid splashed into the water before Johnny could even get a hand on her. He stared over the side of the boat at the place where she had disappeared.

"It's too late," Tanya said, putting a hand on his shoulder. She took the oar from him and began rowing while Johnny slumped against the side of the Zodiac, tears running down his cheeks.

More hybrids leapt from the jetty, grabbing for us as they hit the water. Like last time, they didn't seem to realise when it was time to give up the chase. We were out of reach but they still tried to get us, drowning themselves in the process.

As we rowed farther out, the hybrids stopped, finally understanding they couldn't get us. They stood on the steps and jetty and stared at us with their hateful yellow eyes.

Sam and Tanya stopped rowing and we drifted in the darkness. The wind was picking up. It bit through my clothes and chilled me. The water became rougher. We bobbed up and down on the waves.

"What now?" Jax asked. "I can't get the engine started."

"One thing is for certain," I said, "We can't get around the barricade by going across the harbour. We might have to go around it at the other end, across the bay."

Tanya shook her head. "We'd have to go into those fields. They're heaving with shamblers."

"What if we went over the barricade, man?" Sam asked.

"Climb over it?" I asked.

He nodded. "Yeah."

I looked at the army barricade. The metal wall sections were at least ten feet high and made of smooth steel. If I couldn't get over the wall at the radio station without help, there was no way I could climb over a sheer metal barrier. "We can't get the Zodiac over," I said.

"That doesn't matter," Sam replied. "We can swim to the *Lucky Escape* once we get on the other side. We can all swim." He prodded Johnny Drake. "Hey, can you swim, man?"

Johnny, who had been lost in his own thoughts, looked up and nodded.

"It'll be easy," Sam said.

In the distance, thunder rumbled. I wondered if it was an omen.

"It's a half mile swim," I said, "and the sea's getting choppy."

Tanya looked at me. "Have you got a better idea? It looks like there's a storm coming. If we stay out here with no engine, we'll get washed up on shore and become hybrid chow."

Johnny winced and I realised he was thinking about Cheryl.

Tanya seemed oblivious. "That's not the way I want to go out," she said. "I'd rather take my chances swimming for the boat."

"We could wait for the rain," I said, "and go across those fields when all those shamblers take cover. It's definitely going to rain soon."

"Yes, it's definitely going to rain soon. There's a storm coming." As if to emphasize her point, lightning flashed over the headland. A deep rumble of thunder followed. "We aren't going to be able to row the Zodiac across the bay in a storm. It's miles to the other side. Do you want to row? If we get over the barricade now, we can be on the *Lucky Escape* by the time that storm reaches us."

"Okay, okay," I said, raising my hands in surrender. She was right; there was no way we could row all the way across to the far end of the barricade, especially in a storm.

STORM

Lightning flickered across the night sky again and a cold drizzle began to fall. On the jetty, the hybrids stood glaring at us through the rain, oblivious to it.

I heard something in the distance. A low rumble.

"What's that sound?" I asked.

"It's thunder," Tanya said.

"No, listen."

We all went quiet. The sound of the rain hitting the Zodiac distracted me but if I listened carefully I could hear the distant rumble getting louder.

Worry darkened Sam's face. "It's a boat," he said. "It's coming down the river."

Tanya peered across the water to the mouth of the river. "Do you think the army followed us?"

"Probably," he replied.

Of course the army followed us. We had used their radio broadcast to get our own messages out. We had taken Johnny Drake from them. Did we really think they wouldn't retaliate? Now we were floating in the middle of the harbour while they bore down on us. They would blow us out of the water without a second thought.

The boat appeared at the mouth of the river. The same size as the *Lucky Escape*, it was painted dark green and had searchlights mounted on the top of the bridge. Their powerful beams cut through the night in a wide arc, skimming across the waves towards the moored boats and the jetties.

"What are we gonna do, man?" Sam asked. His voice was tight, frightened.

We had nowhere to run. We could easily swim to shore from here but the hybrids would tear us to pieces. If we stayed on the water, we would be killed or captured by the army.

"We'll have to swim for the shore," Tanya said. If she was nervous, it didn't reach her voice.

"The hybrids..." I said

"There's no other option, Alex. Unless you'd rather be shot."

I shook my head and grabbed my bat.

"Let's go," Tanya said, sliding gracefully into the water and pulling herself towards the shore with a strong breaststroke.

Sam threw down the empty rifle and picked up his tire iron. "See you guys on the *Lucky Escape*." He jumped into the harbour and front crawled after Tanya.

What did he mean by that? Was it every man for himself now? We had more chance as a group. We could fight better as a unit. Alone, we would be hunted down and killed.

I looked over at Jax and Johnny.

"Let's stick together," Jax said.

I nodded.

We lowered ourselves into the cold water and swam slowly for the shore. I was in no hurry to get killed. Ahead, Tanya and Sam climbed out of the water, ran up the sandy incline to the parking area, and sprinted between the buildings.

"They made it," Jax said.

Behind us, the rumble of the army boat seemed to fill the air. The light swung across the harbour buildings and over the jetty, illuminating the hybrids.

Then I heard the death rattle of a machine gun and our Zodiac was torn to shreds.

There was no doubt about the army's plans.

They wanted to kill us.

The search light found us and the blinding beam cast a circle of light around Jax, Johnny, and me.

Bullets tore into the water next to my face.

We weren't going to make it out of the harbour alive.

Twenty-nine

I HEARD ONE OF THE soldiers on the boat shout, "Get us closer!" and I knew he was taking aim again. He wouldn't miss a second time.

I glanced back over my shoulder but the light was too bright to make out anything more than the looming bulk of the boat. In an effort to get closer to us, the pilot steered the craft closer to the jetty.

He obviously had no experience of hybrids and did not know how they behaved when their prey was nearby.

They leapt from the jetty onto the boat. I heard someone shout, "What the fuck? No!" The last word became a scream then died instantly.

The machine gun fired again but the gunner had turned to aim it at the attacking hybrids.

More screams came from the boat. The gun went silent. Smoke and the smell of cordite drifted over the water.

"We need to move now while the hybrids are distracted by the boat," I whispered to Jax and Johnny.

We swam for shore as fast as we could. The screams continued on the boat, mixed with staccato gunshots and shouts of terror.

The hybrids swarmed onto the boat and I was sure nobody was left alive on board. As we emerged from the water and ran for the cover of the military Land Rovers parked near the buildings, I had to reappraise my earlier theory that zombies only bit a vaccinated person once. Maybe that's what shamblers did but the hybrids, who shared the same vaccinated blood as their prey, tore their victims apart and devoured them. I could hear sickening sounds coming from the boat.

I ran for the buildings but Jax whispered urgently, "Here!" She opened the door of a Land Rover and got in. Johnny climbed into the passenger side and I climbed into the back. "The keys were on the dashboard," Jax said. She jammed them into the ignition and started the vehicle.

Turning the steering wheel violently to the right, she turned us around and gunned the engine. A small road led between the buildings and she took it, driving us away from the harbour.

The road intersected with a wider road at a crossroads. Jax turned left.

"Are you sure this is the way?" I asked.

"No, but it should take us back to the water."

The road curved between clusters of tall gas holders then wound towards the sea between tall trees, which bent in the strong wind.

A few splatters of rain hit the windscreen. Jax turned on the wipers. More rain hit the glass at a faster speed until it showered onto the screen so fast the wipers could barely deal with it.

Lightning briefly lit the landscape with a ghostly light then thunder boomed all around us. The storm had begun.

The road opened onto a slim sandy beach. Jax hit the brakes and the Land Rover slewed across the sand, coming to a halt at the water's edge. From this location, the *Lucky Escape* seemed a long way away. The waves were high with white tips.

We got out into the lashing, cold rain. The sea crashed against the Land Rover's tires and the thought of getting into that churning water seemed deadly.

As Jax and Johnny waded into the water, I looked along the slim stretch of wet sand for a boat, any kind of craft that would make the crossing to the *Lucky Escape* easier and less dangerous. What I saw made me rush into the water, joining Jax and Johnny in the ice-cold sea.

Four feral survivors were running towards us, brandishing machetes and big cruel-looking fishing hooks. They were dressed in dark sweaters and waterproof trousers and the look in their eyes was murderous.

I swam for my life, swallowing sea water as the waves pounded into me. The powerful rolling sea and the chill of the water sapped my strength, making it harder for me to keep my head above water. Soon I was gasping for breath between each mouthful of water, coughing to clear my airway. Struggling to survive.

I couldn't see Jax or Johnny. I tried to focus on the *Lucky Escape* but she was so far away and she never seemed to get any closer no matter how much I splashed towards her. Like a mirage, she seemed to shimmer in my vision. I wondered if I was going to black out from lack of oxygen. Maybe sinking down into the depths wouldn't be such a bad way to go. There were definitely worse.

I looked back at the beach. The hybrids had arrived and were feasting upon the bodies of the four feral survivors. Maybe death was preferable to the madness those fishermen had endured, living every insanity-laced day killing others in a frenzy of bloodlust. Now they were at peace. Their apocalypse was over.

I tried to relax, let the insistent rolling of the sea gently toss me over the waves. I kicked my legs and moved my arms slowly, concentrating on just staying afloat. If I got through this, I had to make a sling for the baseball bat so I could put it over my shoulder; its weight and length hindered every move I made.

Lightning cracked the air, followed by a boom of thunder. The rain hit me like a thousand angry needles. I wasn't made for this. My life of exclusively sedentary pleasures was about to catch up with me and send me to a watery death.

I gritted my teeth. I couldn't give up now. I had to see Lucy again, had to believe she had heard my message and would be at the lighthouse. I refused to die before I saw her face again.

Resisting the urge to let myself sink into the dark depths, I let go of the bat and let the waves wash it away so I could concentrate on swimming. My slow breaststroke was bad enough without the hindrance of holding the bat in one hand. I looked up at the *Lucky Escape* and my heart lifted slightly. Her lights were on. Someone had reached her. Probably Tanya and Sam, since I doubted Jax or Johnny could swim that fast.

Tanya and Sam had a head start on us. Maybe the reason I couldn't find a rowboat on the beach was because they had already taken it.

The thought that they were waiting on the *Lucky Escape* for me lifted my spirits. I barely knew these people but we had banded together against a common enemy and helped each other survive. In the face of the zombie and hybrid threat, we had been there for one another.

I hadn't fit into the world before the apocalypse and I certainly didn't fit into it now but these people had helped me, just as I had helped them by thinking up reasons for zombie and hybrid behaviour. That knowledge could help us one day, I was sure of it.

The *Lucky Escape* seemed closer now. I could hear voices calling me from on board. "Come on, Alex. You can do it."

STORM

I was utterly exhausted. The boat was no more than fifty feet away but it might as well have been fifty miles. I pulled myself through the water with the last of my strength but my arms felt dead. I wasn't sure if I was still kicking my legs or not because they were so cold I couldn't feel them anymore.

Somehow I made it to the boarding ladder and grabbed the cold metal rungs. I looked up. The top of the ladder looked so far away. I closed my eyes and conjured up a picture of Lucy's face. If I wanted to see her again for real, I had to get up this ladder.

I pulled myself up and got my boot on the lowermost rung.

Sam and Tanya appeared at the top of the ladder, leaning over the edge of the aft deck, reaching down for me.

"Take our hands, man," Sam said.

I shook my head. At least, I think I shook my head, I wasn't sure. I concentrated on getting my other boot on the next rung. Then the next.

I had to do this myself. If I gave each step every ounce of strength in my body, I could ascend the ladder.

As I got to the top rung, I fell forwards and lay in a pool of saltwater and rainwater on the aft deck, gasping, coughing, and shaking.

I was alive.

And I was determined to stay that way.

I had a job to do.

I had to find Lucy.

Thirty

BY THE NEXT MORNING, THE storm had blown inland, leaving the sky blue and clear. The sun beat down on the *Lucky Escape* and we hung our wet clothes from various railings and lines to get them dry. That meant we were all in our underwear again and I was feeling self-conscious.

I had spent the night shivering naked beneath the blankets in a small bed. Johnny had taken the other bed in the room and curled up beneath his blankets, teeth chattering. Eventually, we had fallen asleep.

Tanya had piloted us out of the inlet and into open water before she, Sam, and Jax took turns sleeping in the second bedroom and keeping a lookout on deck. They wanted to be sure the army didn't send another boat looking for us. The barricade separated us from the river but a radio command from Truro to one of the marinas on the coast could mean a boat being dispatched from this side of the steel wall.

As I sat on the sun deck in my boxers, letting the warm sun heat my skin, I was glad the three had taken such precautions but doubtful there had been any need. The army seemed to be having a huge hybrid problem. We were an annoyance but they had bigger things to think about than four unknown people who had taken DJ Johnny Drake from them.

We had Survivor Radio coming out of the boat's speakers but it was non-stop music. There was no Survivor Reach Out every hour. No dialogue between tracks. Just one song after another.

I had found a notepad and pen on the kitchen counter, with the "Sail To Your Destiny" logo at the top of each page, and as I sat in the sun, I drew a grid on the top page. Two downward lines crossed with two horizontal lines like a tic-tac-toe board.

In the top middle square, I wrote "Zombies". In the top right square, I wrote "Hybrids".

In the middle left square, I put "normal person" and at the bottom left, I scrawled "vaccinated person".

In the squares where the zombies and people intersected, I wrote down what happened when that type of zombie bit that type of person.

Zombie bites normal person; normal person dies and is reanimated as a zombie.

Zombie bites vaccinated person; vaccinated person is bit only once. Wanders away and after four days becomes a hybrid. If approached while turning, will say, "Leave me alone."

Hybrid bites normal person; hybrid kills them and eats them.

Hybrid bites vaccinated person; hybrid kills them and eats them.

Below the grid, I wrote, "Hybrids also kill and eat zombies".

I studied the page for a moment.

What I saw there gave me hope. The hybrids were actually sabotaging the spread of the virus. All it wanted was to spread to as many people as possible and turn them into zombies that would then spread it to more people. The zombies were controlled by the virus and did everything they could to spread it to their prey.

On the other hand, the hybrids seemed to be controlled by a rage that made them kill and eat their victims. They weren't spreading the virus, they were killing potential hosts. They were also killing the zombies.

The arch enemy of the virus was the hybrid.

As more soldiers became vaccinated then bitten by zombies, the hybrid population increased. They were faster than the zombies and appeared to be stronger, so they would eventually decimate the zombie population and the population of living humans. The virus would have no more hosts and no more prey. It would die out.

Unless it mutated.

That was possible. Bacteria and viruses mutated all the time in response to the use of pharmaceutical drugs on patients. If this virus mutated, would it produce something worse than the hybrids? Or would it find a way around the vaccine to kill vaccinated victims and reanimate them as zombies as it did with normal people?

There were too many unknowns, too many variables. I didn't have the knowledge to put it all together.

For now, I had to take hope in the fact that the hybrids were slowing the spread of the virus. Sure, they were doing it by killing everything they could get their hands on but at least it was an effective way to reduce the number of hosts the virus could infect.

I closed my eyes and turned my face to the sun. I couldn't be so clinical about the deaths of all those people when Joe and my parents were in the middle of all this. For all I knew, Lucy might be in danger and not safe aboard *The Big Easy*. I would only know for sure when I got to the lighthouse.

The lighthouse. It was the last place in the world I wanted to go. The memory of Mike and Elena's deaths still stung but I managed to keep it below the surface of my thoughts. I knew visiting the lighthouse would make the memory come swimming up to the surface like a monster from the deep.

Jax came over and sat down next to me. "What are you writing?"

I showed her my grid. "Just some thoughts about the zombies." I told her my theory that the rise of the hybrids could mean the end of the virus.

She thought it over for a while then nodded. "You could be right. But how does that help us right now?"

I shrugged. "It's just a theory. It doesn't help us in any practical way. I don't think there's anything that can kill the virus and stop the zombies and the hybrids. The best we can hope for is that the hybrids kill the zombies then die off eventually."

"That could take years." She looked towards the shoreline. On the cliffs, zombies shambled beneath the morning sun, driven by the virus in their bodies.

"I can't think of any other way this is going to end," I said.

"There are people who know a lot more about the virus than we do," Jax replied. "They could come up with a solution."

"On a secret government island?" I asked, unable to keep the disbelief out of my voice.

She looked at me with a serious expression on her face. "Apocalypse Island is real, Alex. We've known about it for years. The scientists there probably caused this fuck up so they might have a chance of stopping it. The place isn't a joke or an urban legend; it's real. Where do you think the vaccine came from?"

I held up my hands in an attempt to placate her. "Okay, okay. I didn't say the place doesn't exist. If they developed the vaccine, then maybe they can find a cure." It sounded like what she wanted to hear but I wasn't sure I believed it myself. The vaccine, if it had even been developed at Apocalypse Island, did not work. In most cases.

I wondered if there were any vaccinated soldiers who were bitten and recovered completely, without turning into hybrids. It was possible. We wouldn't know about those because they would return to active duty as soldiers. Or maybe they were sent to Apocalypse Island for testing in the hopes of developing a better vaccine. I had no idea. It was all guesswork.

Whether it was optimism or wish fulfilment, Jax needed to believe in Apocalypse Island. I guessed the thought of scientists on an island somewhere, working on a possible solution to the predicament we found ourselves in, was a comfort to her.

My own pessimistic outlook made me think that even if Apocalypse Island did exist, the scientists would only be working in their own best interests, not in the interests of the people stuck on the mainland with the undead monsters.

I didn't say anything to Jax about that. I still had the feeling there was a loved one she was worrying about and I wanted her to be as optimistic about that as she could. I still clung to the thread of hope that Joe and my parents were alive and I knew how thin that thread was. It wasn't up to me to pull another strand from Jax's.

So instead, I said, "Have you got people still alive somewhere on the mainland?"

"I hope so," she said. Tears pooled in her eyes, glistened in the sun. "My boyfriend was at home when the virus spread. I spoke to him on the phone the day before and he said he was going to spend the weekend watching TV with his feet up. I haven't heard from him since. He could be okay. It's not like we live in a big city or anything. We live in a small village in Derbyshire. There's a good chance he's still alive."

"Yes, there is," I said. I hoped for Jax's sake he was. If he was in a village at the time of the virus breakout, he could have holed up there. Or escaped to the countryside. Maybe the army were too busy rounding people up from more populated areas to worry about villages.

But I thought of the village Jax and I had entered, looking for food. It had been empty. Desolate.

"I don't know how I can reach him," she said. "At the moment, going that far inland is too dangerous. Not knowing if he's all right is the worst thing. It's driving me crazy with worry."

I guessed this was where I was supposed to pat her on the shoulder and say, "I'm sure everything will be all right," but we would both know how false that platitude was. Instead, I offered her a weak smile and asked, "What are your plans now that the Survivor Radio mission was successful?"

"We want to find Apocalypse Island," she said. "It was always our plan. If they have some kind of vaccine that actually works, we need to make sure it reaches everyone and not just the authorities."

I raised an eyebrow. "You mean you're going to steal it from a government facility?"

"If that's what we have to do. It's not just the vaccine; they must be working round the clock on other things too. What if they have a vaccine that makes you invisible to zombies like in *World War Z*?"

I rolled my eyes. "I think if they had that, they'd be using it by now, don't you?"

"Okay, so not that in particular but they must be working on other things." The tears were gone from her eyes, replaced with an enthusiastic brightness. I understood then that people like Jax, Tanya, and Sam needed a goal at all times. They were goal-oriented and without that part of their personality being fulfilled, they would probably go as crazy as the feral survivors on the beach.

Although we had banded together, I was the polar opposite from them in a lot of ways. Once I was reunited with Lucy and Joe, I would be happy to take *The Big Easy* out into open water and live a carefree existence on the waves. Fishing. Reading. Listening to music. I could happily adjust to that life while others took responsibility for rebuilding the country from the ashes of the apocalypse.

"What about you?" Jax asked. "What are your plans?"

"Right now, I just need to be reunited with Lucy. After that, I'll take it one day at a time."

"So when we get to the lighthouse, we'll be going our separate ways," she said.

I nodded then asked, "What about Johnny? Is he happy to go on a search for Apocalypse Island with you?"

"Yeah. After his experience at the hands of the authorities, he wants to do anything he can to get back at them."

"Cool. It's weird but I kind of miss hearing him on the radio."

"Me too."

I stood up. "I guess we should get moving. The sooner we get to the lighthouse, the sooner you can start your search for Apocalypse Island."

She smiled and touched my arm. "Thanks for the chat, Alex. Talking to you always cheers me up."

I walked to the bridge ladder wondering if I had mastered the art of conversation…or at least mastered the art of withholding the truth. If I had told Jax what I really thought, I wouldn't have cheered her up at all. Her boyfriend was probably dead and they were crazy to think they could go to Apocalypse Island and set foot in a government facility, never mind steal a vaccine from there and live to tell the tale.

There was a big difference between breaking into a radio station and entering a government facility. The place was sure to be heavily-guarded and not in any half-assed way like the radio station had been.

I was glad I had cheered Jax up but sad that I'd done it by being dishonest.

As I sat in the pilot's seat and started the *Lucky Escape*'s engine, I wondered if I was being dishonest with myself. I had sent out my message on Survivor Radio but there was a good chance Lucy never heard it. We had the radio on nearly all the time on *The Big Easy* but for all I knew, Lucy wasn't even on the boat any longer. There had to be a good reason why she had left me at the marina and it might be that she was taken by the army. They were all over the marina on that foggy day.

My hopes of meeting Lucy at the lighthouse could be nothing more than a mental survival mechanism, the same way Jax and the others had their goals to keep their minds focussed on something other than the hell around us.

What would happen if Lucy didn't turn up? I would never know what happened to her. Would the mental strain eventually send me into madness like so many other survivors?

As I turned the boat south and headed for Land's End, the song on the radio finished and a voice came over the airwaves. Male and smooth and with a mid-Atlantic accent, it said, "Hey, folks, this is Nick Tucker, the new voice of Survivor Radio. We've got lots of great music for all you survivors out there. Don't touch that dial." Evanescence's "Bring Me to Life" started playing.

The army had replaced Johnny Drake quickly.

The world moved on.

Thirty-one

TWO DAYS LATER, WE REACHED the lighthouse. It was mid-afternoon on a cool but sunny day when the rocky island and the lighthouse came into view through the bridge window. Seagulls and crows circled around the island and perched on the railing I had once jumped from to save my life.

Elena had not made that jump.

The tide was in at the moment, so the island was cut off from the beach by a strip of seawater. When the tide went out, a rocky causeway beneath the water would be revealed.

Zombies staggered around both on the island and on the beach. I wanted to take my bat and smash the head of every last one of them.

As we sailed closer, I could see black scorch marks on the rocks where Mike had crashed Harper's boat. Pieces of burnt wood were jammed between the rocks near the water's edge. Charred bodies lay in a blackened mess. Mike's death had been such a waste.

It wasn't until Jax appeared at the top of the ladder and said, "Hey, Alex, we're at the lighthouse. Are you okay?" that I felt my throat hitch and tears sting my eyes.

She came up onto the bridge and put an arm around me. "Hey, it's okay. I'm sure they were great friends and coming here is going to make their loss all the harder. You come down to the living area and have a cup of tea while we wait for Lucy to arrive."

I dropped the anchor and killed the engine. When the rumbling of the engine died, I could hear the distant low moans of the zombies by the lighthouse.

In the living area, I sat on the seat by the window, looking out over the calm sea. Sam handed me a mug of tea and when I took it from him, I noticed my hand was shaking. What if Lucy never showed? How long would we wait before we moved on and I never saw her again?

The tea was hot and sweet as it burned down my throat. I placed the mug on the coffee table and resumed my watch out of the window.

Johnny spoke. "I'm sure she'll come, Alex. You just have to give her time, my friend."

They all knew that Lucy and I were close friends but I hadn't told them just how much she meant to me. I hadn't even admitted to myself how deep my feelings were.

If Lucy didn't arrive, I wasn't sure I could go on without her.

Jax sat next to me. "We'll wait here as long as it takes, Alex. We'll—"

"She's here!" I said, getting up and going to the aft deck. I had seen a boat approaching from the north and I knew it was *The Big Easy*. I recognised her like an old friend I had not seen for too long.

I reached the aft deck and leaned out over the rail. She was coming slowly along the coast, close to the rocks. If the tide was out, she would be too shallow, in danger of grounding herself on the bottom. Lucy knew better than that. What was she doing?

I shielded my eyes against the mid-afternoon sun and peered at the bridge window. I couldn't see Lucy. *The Big Easy*'s bridge was deserted.

The joy I felt at seeing the boat plummeted into a cold pit in my gut. Something was wrong. I rushed up the ladder to the bridge and started the *Lucky Escape*'s engine. Raising the anchor, I turned the boat around and put her on a slow course towards *The Big Easy*.

Tanya, Jax, Sam, and Johnny came out to the aft deck.

"Something's wrong," I shouted down to them, "Something's wrong."

Where the hell was Lucy?

I brought the *Lucky Escape* around in a wide arc and came up behind *The Big Easy*, matching her speed. Through the binoculars, I inspected her bridge.

The wheel had been lashed with a cord to keep the boat on a straight course.

The pilot's seat was empty.

I slid down the ladder to the aft deck. "Tanya, take the wheel and get us closer. I'm going to go on board."

She nodded and went up to the bridge. She did a good job. Within a minute, we were alongside *The Big Easy* and I was able to jump across the narrow gap separating us.

"Lucy?" I called once I was on the familiar aft deck. "Are you here?"

No reply.

I went up to the bridge and untied the cord holding the wheel steady. If I didn't take her out into deeper water, she would be stranded on the sea bed at low tide.

I didn't know what was happening. Lucy had obviously lashed the wheel and set a course for the lighthouse. Only she knew the place I was referring to in the radio message.

But where the hell was she?

I took *The Big Easy* into deeper water and dropped anchor. On the *Lucky Escape*, Jax, Sam, and Johnny watched from the aft deck, worried looks on their faces.

I went down the ladder and into the living area. There, on the table, was a note from Lucy, written in black pen on a piece of paper. I recognised her handwriting but it looked like it had been hastily written.

"Alex. Bitten at 1100 hours on 15th. Lucy."

I didn't understand. Today was the 15th. Was she saying she had been bitten today? Why leave me a note? Where was she?

"Lucy!" I called. "Where are you?"

I heard a noise from below. A low moan?

If she had been bitten this morning, she would have turned by now. No. Please, no.

I didn't even think about taking a weapon with me as I went down the steps to the bedrooms. How had she been bitten? What if she was turned…gone? The note didn't make any sense. If she was leaving me a note to tell me she had been bitten, why write the exact time? What difference did that make? She wasn't thinking straight. With the virus in her blood, she was confused. Perhaps she had been in some kind of denial.

I listened at the bedroom door but everything down there was quiet.

"Lucy?" I whispered. "Are you there?"

Nothing.

I opened the bedroom door, ready to flee back up the steps and jump over the side of the boat if I had to.

The bedroom was empty.

I heard a noise coming from the storeroom.

I pressed my ear to the wooden door and listened.

Rapid breathing came from the other side of the door.

"Lucy," I whispered.

A noise like scuffling on the floor.

I took a deep breath and opened the door.

She lay in the corner of the room, among a pile of T-shirts and the spear guns. She was curled up in an embryonic position, shivering and sweating. Her breath came in ragged gasps. Her jeans were torn on the right thigh. Lucy had bandaged a wound there but blood seeped through the cotton and stained the denim.

Lying next to her on the floor was an empty hypodermic needle. Traces of the amber fluid it had once contained lined the plastic tube.

Now I knew why the time she had been bitten was in the note. She had injected herself with vaccine a few hours ago and knew by the time she arrived here, she would be in this state, unable to tell me what had happened.

The note was a plea for help.

She had four days before she became a hybrid.

She wanted me to try and save her.

I knelt down next to her and reached out to stroke her matted blonde hair.

She shrank away and groaned three words that chilled my heart.

"Leave…me…alone."

Coming Soon
Wildfire

Join the Harbingers of Horror mailing list and get an email when new books come out. http://eepurl.com/OKFY9

You can find all of Shaun Harbinger's books on Amazon here:
http://www.amazon.com/Shaun-Harbinger/e/B00IDCALFQ

Printed in Great Britain
by Amazon